THE FALL

BURNING SKIES

BOOK 1

DEVON C FORD

Published by Vulpine Press in the United Kingdom in 2018

Cover by Claire Wood

ISBN: 978-1-910780-88-6

www.vulpine-press.com

Dedicated to SJ, my military advisor: a man of bountiful knowledge and fearsome facial hair.

NOW I AM BECOME DEATH, THE DESTROYER OF
WORLDS.

J. ROBERT OPPENHEIMER, FROM THE BHAGAVAD GITA

[OF A NUCLEAR WAR:] THE LIVING WOULD ENVY
THE DEAD.

NIKITA KHRUSHCHEV

PROLOGUE

Friday 12:30 p.m. - New York Stock Exchange

Cal walked quickly around the corner onto Wall Street in a state of shock, eyes darting left and right but returning to focus resolutely on the ground in front of him. The uniformed police officers were dashing back and forth, guns raised toward an unseen threat, dealing with casualties, and shouting into their radio mics without success.

All around him people were running and shouting. A screech of tires and a loud smash from behind, echoing from another street, made him jolt instinctively as he glanced back to see a pillar of smoke and flames rising over the roofline of an ornate stone building. Glancing up and behind him, he saw another pillar of smoke and dust, which he guessed was four or five streets away, and the cause of this first rush of desperate foot traffic to escape the area. A uniformed soldier, a national guardsman, thumped bodily into him as he looked away. The soldier looked very young, and scared. Almost as scared as Cal felt.

Returning his eyes to the gray concrete in front of his feet, he sped up as much as the crowded street would allow, his rapid breathing competing for space in his ears over the chaos and multiple sirens. Reaching the access to the subway station, the only way he knew to get back to his hotel and not wanting to check the map of the unfamiliar city he had in his back pocket, he joined the back of a pushing, shouting crowd trying to get below ground.

His genetic code, that of being British, dictated that he could not push through the crowd to get to the front; the unwritten rules of queueing were blindly followed the world over and even more so during a crisis. He was thirty or more pushing, shouting, and panicking people back from the green metal railings funneling the mass of bodies below street level.

He was far enough away to escape the main impact of the blast, but close enough to suffer horribly.

It started as a low rumble, as though the street under his feet was growling at the chaos above, and rapidly became an impossibly loud crack followed by a roiling cloud of dust and black smoke and pieces of debris ejecting from the top of the staircase leading down. The half-dozen people at the threshold of underground and over-ground were catapulted upwards and backwards, their clothing smoldering where it hadn't been torn clean away from the heat and the flames of the blast.

Cal was flattened on his back, cracking his head painfully on the hard ground. He lay there blinking, deafened, trying to make sense of the huge pressure wave he felt before he saw body parts erupt over his head. The concussive wave, the incredible pressure change he felt, had hurt every organ in his body as though they had all been forcibly relocated. Looking up at the tops of the tall buildings in silence—not complete silence but a high-pitched shrieking in his ears—he watched as the slow-motion dark cloud of boiling, black smoke billowed out of the underground portal which so many people saw as a sanctuary from the disorder above.

The stench of the explosion—like rotten eggs and burning plastic—caught in his throat and made him convulse in a racking, gagging coughing fit, which he felt but could not hear. Struggling to his feet, he staggered and wavered until he steadied himself.

In the gaps between the skyline of buildings, he saw similar pillars of dark smoke rising from other explosions across the city.

Inside of thirty minutes, his miserable solitude had become abject terror.

He turned and fled as fast as he could, shuffling on unsteady feet and resolutely sticking to the middle of the street amongst the terrified crowds, hopefully keeping himself away from any other blasts he might come too close to.

SOLITUDE IS PLEASANT, LONELINESS IS NOT

Tuesday 10:30 a.m. - London Heathrow Airport, 74 hours earlier

"To your knowledge," said the bored-looking young woman behind the counter, "has anyone placed anything in your luggage without you knowing?"

She didn't make eye contact with him, and he doubted if she even cared about his answer. He also doubted that she would appreciate him asking her how he would know if someone had put anything in his luggage without his knowledge, as he obviously wouldn't have knowledge of it.

"No," he replied simply, keeping his passive aggressive sarcasm shut up tightly.

The young woman, apparently called Haylee—quite why people were choosing to spell their children's names phonetically nowadays was beyond his comprehension—finally made eye contact with him through layers of thickly applied makeup and smiled falsely. Hidden behind a dense row of fake eyelashes, her eyes didn't mirror the smile as she handed him his boarding pass and directed him toward security.

Yeah, Cal thought to himself, *I'd be bored as shit doing your job too.*

Boarding pass and passport in hand, backpack over one shoulder, he shuffled toward the back of the queue to be directed through a gate only to wait in line again until he was called forward to strip himself of anything metallic.

Shoes, phone, belt, loose change, wallet, watch all went into the dull, gray plastic tray on the squeaking rollers in front of him as a suspicious, but equally bored-looking, security guard eyed him coldly. The last item from his pocket, a small dark box wrapped in velvet, nestled securely alongside his other possessions.

"Any computers/laptops/tablets in your hand luggage?" the guard asked autonomously as he put his backpack in a separate tray. With a sigh, Cal opened the bag and removed the tablet, only to be asked to place it in the tray next to the bag.

His anger and irritation bubbled just below the surface at the pointlessness of this; being treated like a terrorist because he didn't know he had to have his bag and iPad scanned separately irked him, but then again everything got on his nerves recently.

Despite going through wearing only socks and with empty pockets, he still set off the metal detector and was subjected to a personal search, having a hand-held metal detector waved pointlessly fast over his body and having his shoes swabbed. Finally, doing the rushed dance that all Brits did in airport security, he tried to put his belt and shoes on whilst simultaneously stuffing things back into his pockets in haste so as not to cause any disruption to the person behind him in line.

He shuffled through the snaking aisles of the duty-free shopping, ignoring all the offers for the latest fragrance to be doused over him and the slightly cheaper alcohol, and pulled up a stool at the nearest bar and ordered himself a breakfast beer.

After all, he was supposed to be on his honeymoon.

The girl serving his pint looked similarly bored to the girl on the check-in desk and the security guards, and served him wordlessly as the price showed up on a small digital screen in front of him. He paid the exorbitant price with his card by waving it over the card reader and regarded the swirling bubbles of his cheap lager; cheap anywhere except in an airport bar on the wrong side of security. For what he paid for a single pint he could've bought six cans from the shop near his house.

Sod it, he thought again, *I'm on my holidays.* His hand absent-mindedly went to his pocket and to the small box. He retrieved it and ran it between his fingers, pausing with his thumb in the crease to pop open the spring-loaded lid. Instead, he clasped it in his fist and thrust it back into the pocket.

Finishing his beer, he nodded to the unfriendly bartender and stepped down from the stool. He wandered to yet another uncomfortable seat at his departure gate not relishing the eight-hour flight. He looked down at the folded paper in his hands and smoothed it out to reread his itinerary for the hundredth time. She had always organized these things, so he was swimming in the dark by doing it alone.

The printed sheet showed details of the outbound flights, complete with the seat allocation, for Mr. Owen Calhoun and Miss Angela Holt. She should have been Mrs. Angela Calhoun by now, but when they booked their honeymoon—her choice of destination, not his—they had to use their names as they were, not how they were going to be, but she would never be Mrs. Calhoun now.

He was broke, having been strong-armed into exhausting his entire savings on both the wedding and the honeymoon, all of which was non-refundable, non-returnable, and a total goddamned waste of time and money.

As the electronic board changed above him, he saw the other waiting passengers rushing to be first on board.

Sheep, he thought nastily, *all the seats are allocated and it's not like the bloody plane is going to leave without you.*

Shuffling with resigned feet, he joined the line of excited holidaymakers and stressed businessmen and women, the latter making their final calls and texts as the queue inched forwards.

Handing over his passport and boarding pass to another young woman struggling under the weight of multiple coats of makeup, he saw her opening her mouth to inform him that not everyone in his party was present. Seeing the sad look of veiled hostility on his face, she closed her mouth and silently handed back his documents after scanning them, flicking her eyes and her best corporate airline smile to the person behind him.

"26E," said the flamboyant and ebullient male member of cabin crew with a flash of brilliantly white teeth as he handed back Cal's boarding pass and waved him forward. He found his seat, retrieved his tablet and headphones, and stuffed his backpack under the seat in front to save the annoying ritual of getting his bag back from the overhead lockers at the other end. He strapped himself in and shot an unkind look to the empty 26F next to him.

Bitch, he thought, before putting in one earphone and swiping open the tablet to pass the time with a book and some music.

Tuesday 10:40 a.m. – Near Underwood, Upstate New York

Over 3,500 miles away from Cal's plane as it soared upwards to turn west and cross the Atlantic, crossing the Dix mountain wilderness, a man in faded but pressed military fatigues drove a pickup along a rutted track through the woods, kept clear of snow by the heavy tree canopy.

Leland Puller's eyes darted to his rearview mirror intermittently, his counter-surveillance training being second nature after spending his entire adult life honing them into something more intrinsic than a skill. He had been alert the whole time travelling north on Highway 87 before hitting the off-ramp and heading west into the wilderness.

As he often did, being infinitely more careful travelling to their headquarters compound hidden in the woods, he stopped the truck and got out, leaving it blocking the trail just around a sharp bend obscured by the heavy tree line.

He hefted his rifle from the passenger footwell and moved quickly into the woods, legs pistoning efficiently until he was on high ground with line of sight on the road.

Anyone following him would round the bend and be trapped. If he didn't recognize the vehicle or the occupants, he would unload the AR15's entire magazine, slap in another, and empty that too. There would be no warning, no questioning. Even if it was a genuine mistake and he gunned down some lost hikers, then that was just too bad. The sign on the track told anyone who could read that this was private property, and that firearms were in use there.

After ten minutes without sight or sound of anyone, he made his weapon safe and clambered back down to the cab of his truck. He stole a whimsical glance upwards, knowing that the heavy tree canopy would shield him from any prying eye in the sky.

The truck itself was legal, fully registered, as were the AR15, the Springfield in the pancake holster on his right hip, and the Ruger in the ankle holster on his left leg. If stopped by law enforcement he would keep his hands on the wheel and calmly declare to the officers that he was in possession of weapons, which he held valid permits for, and, after they had found he was doing nothing wrong, they would let him go on his way.

Carrying on along the bouncing track, he turned uphill and crested a rise which would ground anything but a tough off-road capable vehicle, before dropping down into the headquarters of the Free America Movement.

They naively believed themselves to be patriots: carefully selected, checked, courted, and recruited.

Almost all of the inner-sanctum members were former or, in some cases, still serving in the military, experts in so many numerous fields that they were effectively a small covert army by themselves. Over the years they had absorbed other organizations, small militias from various towns and cities, and held territory in a half-dozen states.

The second layer of their organization held positions of power or influence, as well as performing job roles in key locations such as working for the power grid and in airports.

They made no noise about their organization or their goals. They posted no vitriolic videos on social media, and the Department of Homeland Security had no idea who, or what they were.

They were off-grid, off the radar, and on-mission.

Leland drove toward the collection of single-story buildings and killed the engine, sliding the gear lever into park. Men and women milled around the camp, dressed similarly and all busy. Leland skirted the large satellite dish on a raised dais of concrete and walked into a wooden hut.

"Morning, Leland," said the gray-haired but robust man sat behind a desk, his broad Boston accent dripping with comfortable confidence.

"Morning, Colonel Butler sir," replied Leland, stiff military obedience and respect for senior ranks as ingrained in him as his counter-surveillance skills were. He didn't salute, as Colonel Butler demanded the Movement soldiers no longer did so after his retirement.

The two men had never served together, even though both had been in-theatre at the same time in both Iraq and Afghanistan. Pullen was in his late-forties and Butler closer to sixty but both men were still fit and formidable. Leland Pullen, former Gunnery Sergeant in the United States Marine Corps, regarded the man before him with something approaching awe.

Colonel Glenn Butler, US Army, retired, was a bitter man behind his smile. He had served his life as a soldier, risen quickly to the rank of colonel and resented that the higher echelons of military command never saw his full potential. He often remarked that had he been promoted to general and been given control of troops in a war zone, then he could have easily defeated any enemy. He saw himself as a role model, a father figure to his boys, and a shining light in the future of his blessed United States of America. He was, although he hid it well, a megalomaniac with a destructive impulse to cleanse his country and purge all the perceived evil influences from it.

"I need you to head to the city, son, get our ducks in a row," he said, rising from his chair and wasting no time on small talk.

"Yes, sir," replied Leland, eager to comply before he fully knew what task was required of him.

"I have someone else overseeing phase one." He paused, not needing to explain that he wouldn't give their name due to OpSec—Operation Security. "And I want you to head up phase two. You know the details?"

Leland did know the details. There were, as they spoke, a hidden army of Movement soldiers in the city ready to perform their role in the revolution.

"Good," replied Butler. He leaned his gaze around Leland and shouted toward the door. "Suzanne?" he yelled. Seconds later the door opened and a woman walked in. Leland knew little about her, other than the fact that she wasn't ex-military but worked in an office which dealt with building planning permissions and regulations before she abandoned the decadent city lifestyle and devoted herself to the Movement. She wore cargo trousers and a drab green T-shirt with a heavy sidearm strapped to her right thigh.

Suzanne handed Leland a Manilla envelope, which he took and guessed it held all but twenty sheets of paper. She nodded to him, smiled, and left the room.

Colonel Butler sat at his desk again, leafing through papers as his attention was already moving on to the next item on the agenda.

"Your contact details are in there," he told Leland, "and, son?"

"Sir?" he said, turning back from the door with his hand paused on the handle.

"We are T-minus seventy-two hours and change until Go. Make us proud," he told him over a steely gaze.

"Yes, sir," he said simply, returning to his truck to make the 250-mile journey to New York City.

~

Just after Leland left the Movement headquarters, Suzanne changed into a smart skirt and jacket over a white blouse, suggestively left with one button too many undone. She knew how to blend in, and how to be seen by men at the same time. She was driven out of the woods by another fit-looking young man in fatigues to the town of Underwood, where she got out and switched her muddy boots for a pair of glossy high heels.

Climbing into an anonymous-looking dark sedan, she adjusted her seat and mirrors, checked the sun visor for the relevant documentation for her lease of the car, reapplied an additional layer of lipstick, and drove south.

LIFE IS A MACHINE SET IN MOTION BY MONEY

Tuesday 2 p.m. – Steakhouse in Albany

Suzanne Emmerson, formerly of the New York State Department, perused the menu in the steakhouse near the Hudson River as she sipped her vanilla latte and waited casually for her guest. As much as she was dedicated to the cause, to the overthrow of a modern society that was so accepting that it practically welcomed terrorists into their towns and cities, she still enjoyed the small luxuries in life when she had the opportunity. Camp coffee and steak got boring after a while.

A nervous-looking young man entered clutching a battered leather satchel a little too tightly and scanned the room. Suzanne saw him come in as she had strategically asked the waitress for a booth offering her a clear view of the only entrance and exit. She waited until he saw her and put on a broad, fake smile and waved at him as she stood.

She disliked the man. He lacked the vision of the men she was used to, and she looked down on him as a man who wouldn't survive without fast food and internet access. Still, she—*they*—needed him, so she played nice.

15

"Hi!" she exclaimed, maybe a little too happily making up for her distain for the weak man. "How was the drive? How have you been?" she said, making their meeting seem innocuous to anyone who may be listening.

The man mumbled his responses, sullen and bitter as he had been for so many years that it became his personality.

The man, Quentin Aaronson, sat but still held tightly to his bag. A look of warning over a smile flashed from Suzanne's eyes.

The message was clear: relax.

He had no idea how her group had found him, how they knew so much about him, but if he was honest with himself, he didn't really care. He had been forcibly ejected from MIT, marched off campus by security, and sent home in shame. Scientific journals, which once heralded him as a genius in the making, now shunned him. He was reduced to returning to his hometown, Boringsville Nowhere, and to a low-paid job repairing electrical items. He was forever known as the boy who threw away a career selling drugs to make his living expenses more manageable. He did not come from a rich or influential family, and nobody spoke up in his defense, so he served two years in a minimum-security state correctional center in Plymouth before returning to his parent's house, having wasted the most promising years of his life and ruining any future prospects.

Now, this woman, who had walked into the store where he worked six months ago and offered him money—enough money to really make a difference—was there to collect.

Ordering herself a salad as a reprieve from the diet of fresh meat she usually lived on, she sipped her second latte and looked at him. He ordered a regular coffee with steak and eggs, well done.

"You can put the bag down," she said quietly through her smile as the waitress walked away. Quentin relaxed and carefully placed the bag beside him. He knew it wouldn't detonate just as well as she did, but the unit he had brought in to show her was still delicate and he didn't want to damage it.

"You didn't have to bring one in here," she said softly as she looked out of the window and over the highways to where the Hudson River flowed out of sight.

"I thought you wanted a demonstration?" he said with a smile. He may not feel comfortable in dealing with her and the people she represented, incorrectly assuming that he was supplying arms to an organized crime group, but his wounded pride dictated that he should earn the ridiculous sum of money she was going to give him. She smiled in response.

They sat in silence until their food arrived, then they ate in silence. Suzanne had no great desire to hear the peevish young man lament about how unfair his life was.

"Can I get you guys anything else?" asked the annoyingly perky waitress.

"No thanks, honey, just the check please," Suzanne answered. She left the table and returned shortly afterwards with a folded piece of paper. Suzanne looked at it, seeing the handwritten thanks signed by Gabby, who had put three kisses on the paper in the vain hope that she would get a bigger tip.

Suzanne paid the thirty-eight-dollar sum with two twenties, ignoring the attempt to illicit extra cash for someone she saw as simply doing their job. Quentin regarded her quizzically, not that she left such a small tip but more that he rarely saw anyone pay in cash any more.

"We don't do plastic," she told him, understanding his look.

"Do you do cell phones?" he asked her, retrieving his own from a pocket and holding down a button to switch it off before slipping it, along with his watch and wallet, into a thick bag.

"No," she said, "we don't."

"Good," he said, before wordlessly reaching into the satchel and audibly flicking a switch.

It was the strangest sensation, to be at the epicenter of a bomb blast without the bomb part. As one, the lights and the music in the restaurant blinked out. The coffee machine, a weaponized array of chrome spouts hissing steam, went slowly quiet. People looked around, checked their dead phones, and the ambient conversation grew louder as people asked what had happened.

Smiling to each other, Quentin and Suzanne rose from their booth and left. Walking side by side into the parking lot, Quentin pointed to a battered old car which he swore to himself would go as soon she paid him the rest of the money. He opened the trunk with the keys, flicked back a blanket and uncovered a dozen other devices like the one he had used in the restaurant. Nestled in between them was a similar device, only twelve times larger and already seated inside a wheeled suitcase as per her instructions. He handed her a sheaf of paper with the handwritten instructions for the devices and smiled, waiting for his money.

Suzanne casually glanced around the parking lot. She had intentionally left her rental car in the darkest corner, and now gestured for him to follow her. She hit the key fob and the four-way lights flashed once to indicate that the car was open.

"It's in the trunk, tucked right back in a black bag in case I got pulled over," she told him. His excitement was palpable and he could barely keep his feet still. Half a million dollars was in the trunk of that car, and it was his.

He was so excited that he didn't notice the heavy plastic sheeting in the trunk, nor did he have any idea that he poked his head inside where there were no witnesses, and no cameras.

Silently, Suzanne withdrew her small silenced weapon, a World War II era 'Hush Puppy,' from her handbag, pressed the muzzle to the back of his head to minimize the flash in the dying light, and pulled the trigger. She caught his legs as his body slumped and tipped him all the way in, taking the car keys from his pocket in the process. She quickly pulled a heavy trash bag over his head and pulled it tight around his neck, wrapping a strip of tape she had placed on the trunk lid around it.

Satisfied that the blood and brains wouldn't leak too much, she shut the trunk and locked the car. She glanced round again quickly, her breath misting in front of her face as she breathed rapidly, and saw that nobody had noticed the interaction. She placed the keys to the rental under the driver's side front wheel and climbed into Quentin's car.

"Fucking lemon, just my luck," she muttered to herself as she moved the stale-smelling driver's seat and drove out into traffic.

An hour north of the city, she pulled in to a rest stop and left the car running. She climbed into the passenger side of the same truck, which had dropped her in town hours before and was chauffeured back to base. There was nothing, not a trace, of her or their involvement in what would be the slow-moving investigation into the disappearance of a nobody with a criminal record for drug dealing. They had never made contact through any electronic means, nothing could be traced to her, and the rental car would be returned wearing its original plates after all forensic traces of the dead body had been removed.

Behind her, well-spaced and aware of any possible, however unlikely surveillance, drove the dark sedan. The EMP devices, the lemon she had driven and the sedan containing the body of Quentin Aaronson had disappeared from her life, Suzanne didn't know where to—OpSec—but she had done her part. For now.

"MOST CITIES ARE VERBS; NEW YORK'S A NOUN."

Tuesday 8 p.m – Waldorf Astoria Hotel

Cal had read that quote by John F. Kennedy written on a wall somewhere before he dragged his suitcase into the grand lobby of the hotel. He was sure his mood had something to do with it, but he simply wasn't feeling it.

His anger at doing this alone was killing him; all he had wanted was somewhere hot with a beach, a pool, and a bar. He could have spent two weeks in Spain—all-inclusive—for less than this hotel had cost him for five days. That had been Angie's fault too. She had demanded they have a city break in New York for their honeymoon so she could shop and he could see the sights, and now she was nowhere to be found.

So there he was alone in New York and feeling, not for the first time, like a young Macaulay Culkin only without the fun.

He paused as he entered, marveling at the immaculately patterned carpets, the acres of dark wood and golden gilt detailing on the high ceilings. A uniformed bell hop sprang forward to reach for his case with an expectant smile. Looking every part the tourist, Cal walked toward the shining reception desk being followed by his luggage where a woman in a uniform, which looked more expensively tailored than the wedding suit he never got to wear, smiled at him.

"Hi there, sir" she said. Her name badge said she was called Bridget.

"Hi," Cal replied, feeling boorish and underqualified to be there. "I have a reservation. Owen Calhoun?"

"Sure thing, sir," Bridget answered, her smile still sparkling at him. "Just let me check the system." Cal waited as she tapped at keys efficiently, stealing another glance around the room and feeling even more out of place as a man probably twice his age walked through the lobby with a stunning girl at least a decade younger than Cal on one arm.

"Congratulations!" Bridget exclaimed, snapping his focus back to the desk. "I see you're here on honeymoon, so we'll bring a bottle of French champagne on ice up to your room shortly," she went on, still smiling and completely failing to register his teary-eyed look of violence as she also failed to grasp that the guest's wife was nowhere to be seen.

"Can I have someone take your bags up to your room Mr. and Mrs. Calhoun …?" she said, trailing away as the smile finally wavered when she registered the look on his face and the obvious lack of a Mrs. Calhoun.

"It's just me," he said, his voice cracking and betraying him. He coughed and started again.

"It's just me. There is no Mrs. Calhoun. And all champagne is French, otherwise it's just fizzy wine," he said petulantly, finally matching his behavior with his feeling of being out of place.

Bridget didn't know what to say, her mouth opening and closing but the public-facing smile still trying hard to stay on point.

"I ..." she began, still smiling but dying under the weight of embarrassment and shame. Cal instantly regretted his harsh words and apologized.

"I'm sorry. It's been a tough couple of weeks," he told her, gaining her condescending sympathy as her 'happy welcoming smile' underwent a corporate metamorphosis into 'dealing with upset guest' mode.

"Well," Bridget said, rebooting and recovering from the mishap "I ..."

"I'll take it from here, Bridget, thank you," said a rich, cultured male voice from behind him.

"Mr. Calhoun," said the voice, making Cal turn and regard an exceptionally well put together man. He was tall, maybe six two, and had the body of a swimmer with hair graying at his temples like it had been dyed that way to make him seem infinitely wiser in the ways of the world.

"My name is Sebastian, I am the concierge here." He placed his left hand on his chest and sketched the smallest of bows, like a man used to greeting people from all over the world. Cal, in contrast to the exquisitely dressed man in front of him, dwarfed in both height and manners wearing scruffy jeans and a T-shirt, held out a hand. Sebastian shook it, holding it in a firm grip and not letting go as he leaned his head to the side to catch Bridget's eye.

"Bridget? Perhaps we can switch out that *French* champagne for a bottle of malt whisky?" he said with a smile, making his orders sound like a polite request.

"Certainly, Sebastian," Cal heard Bridget say from behind him.

"Mr. Calhoun," Sebastian said, "may I call you Owen?"

"Nobody calls me Owen," Cal replied, "call me Cal."

"Okay Cal, walk with me?"

He snapped his fingers and a uniformed bellboy ran forward to take Cal's bags. Sebastian picked up a key card from the reception desk and walked toward the elevators. Cal, relieved of his luggage which disappeared into a separate elevator, found himself swept along with the smooth man as though caught in his wake.

"Whereabouts in England are you from?" Sebastian asked him as the doors closed.

"Home counties," Cal replied. Realizing that someone in New York likely had no idea what he meant so he added, "South of London."

"Surrey or Kent?" Sebastian asked with a small smile, gaining the desired look of astonishment from Cal.

"Surrey. Most people wouldn't know that," he said.

"Cal, most people don't make it their business to know where our guests come from," he said as the doors opened and he stepped out onto more lush, thick carpet.

Handing the key card over, Cal swiped it over the door of the room. Cal walked inside to find, miraculously, his luggage already in the room and a silver tray bearing a bottle of expensive scotch and a pair of crystal tumblers. Sebastian saw the two glasses and furrowed his brow, no doubt analyzing the performance of his staff and finding fault; providing two glasses was an error in diplomacy, but he recovered it.

"Allow me," he said, opening the bottle and pouring two measures. "Welcome to New York City," he said, raising one of the glasses as he offered the toast to Cal. Unable to resist the ingrained manners of an Englishman, he raised his own glass to return the gesture. Sebastian kept hold of the glass he drank from to subtly remove it from the room as though its inclusion were intentional.

"I'll leave you to get freshened up, I'll be in the lobby until ten pm," he said as he turned for the door. "I'll have a reservation made for you at our restaurant, compliments of the Waldorf."

With that, Sebastian left. Cal drained the glass, stripped off his travel clothes and moments later stepped under a steaming shower.

CHANGE THE PLAN, NOT THE GOAL

Wednesday 7:30 a.m. - Washington, D.C.

Major Stephen Taylor of the National Guard placed the empty piece of paper over the one crammed with tightly packed text. Using a simple decoding pad was old-fashioned, archaic even, given the level of technology at their disposal.

Rotating digital encryption keys would allow the different factions of the Movement to speak freely, but the colonel was very specific; the enemy held those encryption keys as much as they did.

"We keep it old-school, son," Butler had told him. "Keep those ass-hats guessing."

The ass-hats he referred to were predominantly the Department of Homeland Security, not to mention the NSA, the FBI, and local police departments, and those shady sons-of-bitches working for the Department of Defense who answered to nobody but Washington. Taylor had once asked him about the CIA, and the big man had enigmatically told him not to worry about the goddamned CIA with a smile.

DHS and their seemingly unending powers, however, did concern him. Absolutely no member of the Movement used a mobile device to contact one another. No emails, no text messages, no using any cell phone connected to the Internet. They met face-to-face when they could, and communicated nothing via the airways.

"We go dark, boys," Butler had said. "Keep them guessing."

So they communicated in slow time, with truckers delivering sealed envelopes up and down the country, but slow in this case meant utterly safe, utterly insulated, and utterly anonymous. Even an intercepted message would take some linguistic genius sat at his desk in Quantico months to decipher every possible meaning of the message without an encryption pad, and even if they were successful, the intel would be so old as to be worthless to them anyway.

Taylor read the message again. He was unhappy, and the colonel was most definitely unhappy, because he had failed.

```
Maj. Move past the problem and find a
solution. Destroy or disrupt target by
any and all means necessary. Time of
execution remains unchanged. Make it
happen.
```

Taylor hated failure. It galled him. He was a professional soldier and he had a duty; a duty to his country, to his commanding officer—of the Movement, not the spineless jerk he had to report to—and above all he had a duty to his men.

The malfunction and loss of their own 'pinch' bomb, of their EMP device, was the fault of nobody but still it had happened. They still had a mission to undertake, they still had a target, but now they would rely on plans B and C. Major Taylor had cautioned Colonel Butler that a backup plan would put civilians in jeopardy, would likely result in casualties, but the mission remained. He knew his men would do their duty, and they were all prepared to break eggs making this omelet.

His men. They were what mattered most to him.

His men and women, technically, but the females under his command were the last ones to make a gender distinction, unless to point out that they could kick a man's ass just as easily as anyone else. His brigade was well trained, and they looked up to him because he looked after them when they felt that their country no longer cared.

His trusted members of the Movement, a great portion of his fighting strength, were disillusioned servicemen and women, the majority of which found themselves pulled from the frontline and sent home with no time to adjust. They were thrown back into a society torn between looking down on them or thanking them for their service. A good number of his troops were from poor families who had joined up fresh out of high school, and now faced rising unemployment, a total lack of belonging, and conflicting media reports that their God-given second amendment rights would be taken from them by a government they felt was unconstitutional.

They felt abandoned; they needed something to believe in and something to fight for. They were part of the biggest war machine in the Western world, and they were trained to kill. There was little space for people like them back in the world; sure enough some went into law enforcement or the Department of Corrections, the lucky ones went home to families and jobs, but many were just hung out to dry.

So, thought Taylor with resignation, *plan B it is.*

And he made it happen.

Wednesday 9:30 a.m. - 5th Avenue

Cal, having gorged himself on steak and seafood in the exquisite restaurant before washing it down with an entire bottle of red wine, woke with the echoes of a hangover bouncing around inside his skull and ricocheting off the walls of jet lag.

After throwing off the covers in the enormous and impossibly comfortable yet firm bed, he stepped into the waterfall shower again and let the decadence wash away the stress of yesterday. He dressed, ate a big breakfast of pancakes whilst surreptitiously pocketing a few pastries for later—no sense in buying lunch—and headed outside.

He had never seen so many people congregated in one place. Never seen so many cars packed bumper to bumper. Never heard such deafening ambient noise as every sound in the possible world competed for space in his ears under the overriding wail of sirens and car horns.

He swiped across the lock screen on his phone and brought up the map, even though as something of an afterthought he'd picked up a paper map from a stall near the decadent reception desk, which thankfully wasn't manned by Bridget and her fake smile. First stop, which was the nearest, was the Rockefeller Center.

The plan, which had been Angie's plan that he found himself agreeing to, was to see the sights of the famous New York City. Cal still felt bitter about not going somewhere with a beach, among many other things, which made his default position in the world rest at angry, but with the sidewalk under his feet he felt the stirrings of something resembling happiness.

Finding the Rockefeller within minutes, he swiped his phone from map to camera and reversed the lens. Leaning back and holding the phone at arm's length, he grinned his best "I'm having the time of my life" smile and snapped the shot with the iconic buildings in the background.

Done. Get that online later, he thought, *needs a hashtag though ... something like, #whoneedsawife? or #f*ckyouangie?*

Deciding that he had seen the iconic buildings, he felt that they looked too busy and the line of people waiting to pass through a security checkpoint was too long, he changed his mind about going inside. His intention was to see, if not experience, as many of the landmarks as he could to show the world that she hadn't broken him. Switching back to the map, he retraced his steps to hit 5th Avenue again. Almost immediately the building across the wide street from him took his breath away, so much more impressive and attractive than the skyscrapers people talked so much about. The cathedral was packed with people out in front and the sidewalks were cluttered by people trying to take their own picture with selfie sticks. It was like an assault course for anyone trying to just get by. Cal snapped a couple of pictures from his side of the street; even if he'd managed to cross over in one piece he'd end up having to take his own selfie from an angle which would look straight up his nose to get the beautiful building in the frame.

As with so many other people who have never visited a place laid out in a grid, he marveled at the high buildings to either side as his progress was halted for each street he had to cross. His earlier elation at his sense of freedom faded somewhat when he tried to walk casually and enjoy himself. He soon found that acting like a rock in a riverbed was less fun than he imagined, because instead of the people flowing around him like water, he found himself bumped and shoved by every fourth man or woman to walk by him.

He gave up and quickened his pace to that of a New Yorker: hurried. Another six blocks north took him to a towering monstrosity of dark glass. Catching the name over the doors finally forced him to make the perilous journey across the street to take his photo with the sign behind him. He hoped the face he pulled would make people laugh and like it when he posted it later. Slipping his phone back in his pocket he carried on, his eyes peering inside the windows of Tiffany & Co. where a glance at the big diamond rings removed his good mood like a pin connecting with a balloon.

Everywhere he looked people were bustling along, utterly sure of where they were going and in a rush to get there. People shouted into their cell phones or into the small mics in the cables to the earbuds they wore. He was startled the first time he saw the venting steam rising from the street ahead, like some layer of hell waiting just below the surface. He had dressed for colder weather, but soon found that the concentration of people and fumes inside the narrow alleyways of skyscrapers made it warmer than he expected.

Glancing to his right he locked eyes with a man in the back seat of cab. A real *gen-u-ine* NYC yellow cab, as iconic the world over as the bulbous, noisy, and uncomfortable black cabs of London.

Being British and being abroad in an unfamiliar city teeming with tens of thousands of people who all seemed to know where they were going, his embarrassment took over in an instant and he tore away his gaze knowing that he could never look back in that direction for as long as he lived. It was almost as awkward for him as accidentally touching a stranger's hand in a crowd.

Now that he was very aware of the cab next to him, he realized that there seemed to be no point in anyone driving anywhere in New York. For almost six blocks he and the cab leapfrogged each other, both making slow progress through the streets which just didn't seem to have been built with this many people in mind, until blessedly the cab turned off down a one-way street ahead of him.

Now he saw that the buildings ahead to his left dropped away, and the imposing skyline of glass and brick and stone gave way to daylight and the color green, bringing with it a renewed chill in the air. His elation at walking solo in the big city caught up with him, and he realized his feet were already starting to hurt. He had spent more time on his feet in the last twenty-four hours than he usually did in a week, and he placed his ass on the nearest bench in Central Park with a sigh of relief.

He snapped himself another selfie, then retrieved a small pastry from his pocket and ate it, all the while keeping watch on a street preacher yelling on the sidewalk from his left, promising eternal damnation to all who didn't repent their sins. From there he intended to walk through the park, visit the zoo, then head back to his decadent hotel room.

Angie may not have been there, may have ruined his life, but their goal when they booked the honeymoon was to see the city.

The plan had changed, but the goal remained the same.

DUCKS IN A ROW

Thursday 6 a.m. - Free America Movement Headquarters

"Suzanne!" barked Colonel Butler as he returned to his command center following his morning run. Two other Movement soldiers had run through the steep forest trails with him, both men half his age if they were a day, but he had still led the way and dictated a fierce pace which they struggled to match.

"Suzanne!" he called again, annoyed that he had to repeat himself.

"Here, sir," she called out from inside his office. Nodding to his running partners, their misting breath combining to form a steamy cloud enveloping them all, Butler went inside.

"Good morning," she said, handing him a cup of coffee and perching herself on the corner of his desk. Butler chugged down the hot coffee, wiping his mouth with a hairy forearm. Suzanne waited patiently for him to finish, watching as his thick chest rose and fell.

Any normal operations command center would be bristling with wires and screens, radio headsets buzzing and phones ringing, but this was more like the command post of a general in the civil war; runners came and went with information written on pieces of paper and each one was decoded using the same method the Movement used throughout the country. People quietly shuffled the papers, sometimes getting up and calling a runner to take messages out to town where their wider network of contacts would distribute them. There was always a flurry of activity first thing every morning, after that the slow-moving flow of information and intelligence ground almost to a halt until the afternoon brought new information.

The only nod to modern technology at all were six plasma screens mounted on the wall, all of them showing twenty-four-hour news from the US as well as international news. Each was fed through the satellite mounted outside, and it was the only electronic connection with the outside world. The satellite let news in, but nothing out. It was safe, and even Butler was sure that the NSA or Homeland Security couldn't eavesdrop on them through the news channels.

The news, national, international, and local, was the best way to stay abreast of events and come tomorrow, would be his window to the world to see if the plans he had so painstakingly created and nurtured, in some cases over years, were working.

"T-minus thirty hours and change," said Suzanne, as though Butler hadn't been aware of the countdown clock. Bizarrely, she was the only person in the movement not to call him sir or treat him like some kind of mortal god. She was different. She wasn't ex-military, had no military family members—she had no family at all that Butler knew of—and she had no personal axe to grind at the dissolution and disarming of American soldiers. She had carried a 9mm, a purse gun as Butler would call it favoring his heavy forty-five, and went to her local range every so often to keep her eye in. She was no militant, no wounded ex-servicewoman left to rot on a pension too small to keep a roof over her head, but she had found the Movement, she had recruited herself, and she was invaluable to him.

The device clipped to Butler's waist emitted a shrill chirping noise, and prompted everyone around to disappear. This was the only connection via modern telecommunications allowed, and was never used to contact other members of the Movement; calls on this satellite phone were a one-way only thing. When Butler was alone in the room, he flipped up the ruggedized rubber antenna and hit the button to answer the call.

"Butler," he said gruffly. He paced as he listened, nodding to himself and occasionally acknowledging something before he finished with, "Yes, we are on schedule."

The phone was given to him when he was recruited to run the Movement. He believed the person who gave it to him when they claimed to be high up in the CIA, and the flow of intelligence proved to be 100 percent accurate, 100 percent of the time so he had never been given any reason to doubt their integrity. The voice on the other end of that phone had assured him that the encryption software used for their calls was not of US origin, and that no domestic security services could access it. The CIA man had provided funds and munitions, and Butler had never felt like he was a puppet on the end of the strings, but more like he had an equal, a true believer and patriot, helping him achieve his goals.

Returning the phone to his waistband he called Suzanne back in to the room.

"Sir?" she answered as she strode in confidently.

"Get a runner to go to D.C.," he told her. "Taylor's eyes only."

"Replacement EMP?" she asked.

"No," Butler said, unconcerned at the risk of collateral damage. "Plan B. There's a bomb for him to collect."

~

Suzanne had been navigating the desperately dull world of planning and development, and had been a bored woman. She was bored with life, bored with her job, bored of working hard and never actually seeing a difference to the people she felt mattered.

She had harbored this boredom for years, counting down the weeks of her life as just one catastrophic Tinder date and disappointing sexual encounter every Friday at a time. She wasn't there because she really believed in the cause, although she did believe in many things the Movement stood for, but she was there all the same. She was there because she just wanted something, *anything*, to change. She wanted to see the cycle broken. She wanted to find a more fulfilling way to live her life.

The final straw had come when someone from the Office of Professional Integrity walked into her office one morning and shot her a steely, yet almost gleeful gaze as he bypassed her and walked straight into the office of her supervisor, another failed romantic involvement, and shut the door.

Ten minutes passed until her supervisor, a man who felt that wearing a bow tie to work made him seem young and relevant, when in fact it made him look a little like a child molester, smiled a fake smile and asked her if she would kindly join them.

She had packed up her purse, logged off her computer terminal for the last time, walked into the office, and sat down.

"Hi Suzanne," said her boss, desperately hoping that their brief affair didn't become public knowledge as a result of this, "thanks for joining us. This is Mr. Andrews from the—"

"I know who he is," Suzanne interrupted, just about fed up with her life. "Well not who he is, but where he works." She turned to regard the man sat next to her, and he returned her smile. She hated people like that; people who reminded her of snakes and grease, internal affairs people. "I could smell internal affairs when the elevator door opened, and that was before the temperature dropped twenty degrees," she said, silencing the room as the smile on the face of Mr. Andrews dropped off the earth.

"I'll save you the trouble," she said, rising from her chair, "I quit. I haven't taken a holiday in months so I expect my notice to be a paid absence." With that she left the room, leaving both men stunned.

As an afterthought, the door burst open again and she leaned her head back inside.

"And say hi to your wife for me," she told her boss. "Tell her I'm sorry she has to sleep next to you, because I sure as hell didn't enjoy it."

With that, she slammed the door and left an incredibly uncomfortable silence in the room.

"It was just an informal talk about her use of the internet during work hours," said Andrews, openmouthed at the hostility she showed them both. The man opposite him was too shocked, too scared that Suzanne would say something to his wife, to anyone, to answer.

The internal affairs man rose to return to his office, and to tell his boss that the woman had quit before he even had chance to produce his reams of printouts showing when she had been searching the internet for things not related to work activity. He dropped the ream of paper in the secure recycling bin on his way out, saddened that he wouldn't get to showcase how meticulous he had been in counting up all the hours she hadn't been working when at her desk, even if he would get to gossip about the office manager not keeping it in his pants.

If he had taken the time to see what sites she had visited, had bothered to look further than the end of his nose, he may have discovered that Suzanne had been researching off-grid living, had booked herself on a wilderness survival course, had purchased another firearm and items of clothing and equipment a lady working a desk in the Planning Department shouldn't have need of.

But he didn't.

Suzanne went home, gave almost all of her possessions away to Goodwill, listed her house for rental, and sold her car for cash. She forwarded her mail to a PO Box, took a train and a cab to her survival course, and spent two glorious months in the woods where she met one Colonel Glenn Butler and seemingly became an eager convert. She didn't want the ideology, she just wanted the excitement. And she found far more than she had expected to.

LIFE IS A ONE-TIME OFFER

Thursday 8:15 a.m. - Battery Park Ferry Terminal

Cal regretted his decision to book a place on the first ferry of the morning. He regretted his decision this time not to bring a coat, thinking it would be as warm as the previous day, as the wind blew bitterly after he had passed through another airport-style security checkpoint and took his seat. He regretted drinking enough alcohol for two people and eating in the same restaurant as the previous night, and he now regretted booking his ticket through the reception desk and requesting his wakeup call.

When he woke to the sound of the ringing telephone by his ear, he almost cursed down the line and decided to forget the trip.

Lying on his back, tangled in the covers with both eyes covered by his hands, Cal groaned aloud as he accepted that he now had a hangover. The groan deepened and grew in intensity when he remembered how much he had spent on his credit card, not realizing the expensive kindness Sebastian had showed him by granting his first night's meal on the house.

No, he told himself, *get out of bed and experience life.*

He got out of bed, brushed his teeth, and threw on his clothes. Rushing down to the lobby, he rounded a corner and almost cannoned into a man in a suit which cost more than his car back home. Smoothly recovering as though his DNA was coded toward always showing a publicly acceptable face, Sebastian turned to face him.

"Good morning, Cal," he said. "I trust you slept well?"

"Yeah," croaked Cal, "bit hungover to be honest …"

"And yet you're up so early?" Sebastian asked.

"Yeah," Cal said again, "I booked myself on the Statue of Liberty ferry tour and I'm running late."

Sebastian took all this in, placed a hand on Cal's shoulder and deftly steered him away. He glanced over his shoulder to the desk and said, "Lauren, please ask Mike to bring the car around."

Before Cal could say anything, mostly that he couldn't afford a private car, Sebastian steered him toward the coffee machine and poured him a coffee before adding cream and two sugars; how the man knew how he took his coffee was beyond his comprehension and the question struggled to compete in his half-asleep brain for priority, but it was headed off.

"Mike will get you to Battery Park," Sebastian said, holding up a hand to stop any objection. "He isn't needed for an hour, and it's compliments of the Waldorf—"

"I know," interrupted Cal. "Compliments of the bloody hotel. Why are you being nice to me?" he said, instantly regretting the harshness in his voice as he crossed way over into aggressive ingratitude.

"Cal," said Sebastian, patient and calm, "don't argue, just take the car, *sir*."

Cal locked eyes with him, seeing a kindred spirit capable of more kindness than he felt he deserved, and softened.

"I'm sorry," he said, failing to fully convey how he felt, "I'm just angry all the time …"

"I know," said Sebastian, still patient and understanding despite Cal's behavior, "and I'm sure it will pass. Don't you Brits have a saying about looking gift horses in the mouth?"

"Yes," replied Cal, "but I never understood it."

"It means," Sebastian said patiently, "that if you're given something for free, don't check it out like you're buying it. Now take your coffee and get in the limo."

He smiled, turned away and greeted another guest by name, switching into another language with effortless grace. Cal sipped his coffee, good coffee, and walked outside to see a shiny, black town car with a dark-suited man holding the door open.

"Good morning, Mr. Calhoun," he said. "Battery Park shouldn't take us long at this hour." He smiled, gestured Cal into the back of a car he couldn't afford the insurance for, and closed the door after him.

Cal, as grateful as he was for the kindness showed him, did not enjoy the cold and windswept tour around the Statue of Liberty. He was hungover, despite the three cups of coffee he had poured down his neck in standard NATO form of milk and two sugars—a distant memory from his younger days which had become an ingrained habit—and he was suffering. As much as he suffered, he was still pissed that the Ellis Island ferry seemed to offer better views of the Statue. He spent the tour close in under the shadow and constantly craning his neck upwards. By the time the ferry brought him back, complete with his obligatory 'Statue of Liberty in the background selfies' on his phone, he was hungry and he was pissed.

Stopping off at the first hot dog stand he found, he paid cash for two with everything, not that he knew what everything entailed, and ate them both as he walked feeling cheated out of the ten dollars he had just been charged.

I must look like a tourist, he thought.

He knew he was near the monument at ground zero, the site of the former World Trade Center and home to an incredible monument to the fallen, but he couldn't face the sadness he might feel seeing it.

Maybe tomorrow, he told himself.

Feeling better with a full stomach he rode the subway, which he found was an experience unlike any other, and he had used the London Underground more times than he could count. He wasn't prepared for the differences, which were accentuated by his thinking that he knew what to expect. The noise and sheer number of passengers deafened him, and the trains seemed so much louder than he had expected. He had even intentionally missed two trains to stay and watch the incredible street performers in a subway station, after finding himself drawn to the music as though his bad mood needed the company of music. He uncharacteristically dropped money into the collection box and exchanged a happy nod with the front man playing an oversized saxophone.

Eventually, he found himself in Midtown where he stood and marveled, not caring if he looked like a tourist or not, at the gargantuan flashing neon lights of Times Square. Finding quickly that the daylight fireworks display of flashing lights soon lost its appeal, he told himself he had to come back at night to fully appreciate it.

A tall man with a bright yellow snake draped across his shoulders made straight for him, flashing an almost maniacal smile. Cal fought the urge to turn and run, to ignore the strict rules on jaywalking and flee across lanes of busy traffic, but the mood he carried from the subway performers stayed with him and he held his ground, posing for awkward pictures as the huge constrictor wrapped itself slowly around his neck.

A few photos taken on his phone later, taken purely for social media use and to prove to everyone, including his ex-fiancée who he was certain would be indulging in some online stalking, that he was enjoying life, he turned and headed south again.

An hour later, he shuffled in line waiting to get into the Empire State building, taking his tourist headphones and listening to the voiceover of a stereotypical New York cabbie inundate him with facts and history about the tower.

As he rode the long elevator to the top of the world, Cal's ears popped uncomfortably long before he had to get out and move to a different elevator to reach the observation deck.

ORGANIZED CHAOS

Thursday 10:20 a.m. - Manhattan South District

Leland sat in the bland and empty apartment with two Movement soldiers acting as his security detail. The door knocked occasionally and one of the soldiers would admit a man or woman who sat at the small table with him. No names were exchanged, but each gave the code phrase which Leland gave the correct response to.

Another knock at the door and a heavy-set Hispanic man with a fearsome beard entered. He nodded to the man who admitted him, sat down heavily after stomping the wet sludge from his boots, and looked into Leland's eyes. He had the look of a trucker, Leland thought, which made sense.

"Cold for this time of year," the man said woodenly.

"Better weather is on the way," Leland replied, emotionless.

Their exchange held no tone of conversation; it was simply a question and an answer: *Can I trust you? Yes.*

Leland produced a stack of papers and asked the man if he knew his target. He confirmed that he did. Leland asked if he knew the timings. He answered, "Affirmative, Gunny."

A former Devil Dog then, thought Leland. Judging by his age, he guessed the man had probably served in Beirut.

Leland shook his hand before he left, and ticked off a line on his list.

Manhattan, Williamsburg, Queensboro, Kennedy, Willis, 3rd, Madison, West 145th, Macomb's Dam, the '95 in both directions, Washington on both sides of the island, West 207th, Broadway, Hudson Parkway, and all of the tunnels. Only the Brooklyn Bridge was left untouched, by whatever design the colonel intended, but that wasn't his concern.

The logistics of the operation were massive, but the execution was simple.

~

Carlos Rodriguez took the stairs one at a time, the pain in his back returning. He had good days and bad, and recently spending long hours behind the wheel aggravated the old shrapnel wound. He was entitled to disability, but it wasn't enough to live on so he was forced back into work. He got through by trucking, a skill he had obtained in the Corps, and he found himself easily recruited to the Movement.

He had to admit, the plan was brilliant. Stealing C4 and blowing bridges with precision charges would have a high casualty rate, not to mention permanently harm the infrastructure with millions of dollars' worth of damage caused. This way was effective, more temporary, and easily achieved.

Stealing or stockpiling enough explosives to achieve their objective was more than risky; someone would notice, they would alert the authorities and they would likely fail. Rodriguez only knew a small portion of the plan, his higher involvement necessary because he was a key player in obtaining the materials they needed, and for months he had planned his role ready for the following day.

The Movement would look after him and his family, and those Wall Street assholes would find out what life on the other side is like.

Thursday 11:10 a.m. - Empire State Building

Cal was unhappy at spending another $34 on top of the $12 he had spent getting into the zoo the previous day. He read the sign advertising the NY Pass, listing all the attractions it would get him into. By his rough math, he was already going to be out of pocket by paying individually. That was Angie's remit; she had always been the organized one who found the deals online and got them into places at a discount.

Bitch, he thought bitterly again, *still costing me money.*

He paid his fees, went through security, and headed for the top of the building, shuffling his feet during the long elevator ride as they were still hurting him from all the walking he wasn't used to.

The observation deck was packed, and more disappointingly, Cal saw that he was actually nowhere near the top. The place was literally thronging with tourists. The fact that he was a tourist escaped him briefly, and he inched forward to get a good view.

In spite of his dark mood and his aching feet, he had to admit that the view really was something special. The clouds had broken, and, despite the wind chill, he could see for miles. The East River to one side, the Hudson to the other, the Statue of Liberty clearly visible, and a skyline that made his jaw drop, even if all he could see essentially was miles and miles of concrete laid out below adorned with air-conditioning units sprouting from the buildings like so many small parasites. How mankind could cram so much activity, so many people, into a small island was a wonder to him. Getting out his phone he took a few panoramic shots, the resulting pictures jumping from frame to frame as the mass of people made his footing unsteady. He settled on a 360-degree video, overshadowed by the loud commentary in multiple languages, when the crowd began to make a similar noise all at once. He had abandoned the audio commentary, partly because he refused to shuffle along to the relevant numbered boards to be told what he could see, and partly because the borderline-offensive stereotype in his ears annoyed him.

Turning instinctively toward the source of the interest, people around him everywhere broke out into spontaneous applause.

What the fuck? he thought, before a person in front of him shifted position to take a picture of the scene. There, at the top of the goddamned Empire State building, was a man on one knee holding up a ring box to a tearful, emotional, and embarrassed girl.

"Oh, fuck my life!" he groaned aloud before his brain could intercept the words from reaching his mouth.

All around him people tutted and made disapproving noises, heightening his sense of shame. One woman even tapped him on the shoulder.

"You should be ashamed of yourself," she told him. "It's a beautiful thing."

Cal couldn't take it. Wordlessly he pushed through the cooing crowds and headed for the elevator. Remarkably it wasn't too full as he turned himself sideways to disappear into a gap and hang his head. Tears pricked his yes, feeling simultaneously angry and sorry for himself, when a voice behind him spoke.

"I thought it was lame too," it said. Female, rich in humor and sarcasm, and seemingly directed at him. He turned to face the woman who spoke.

Tall, slim, with a ring in her nose under eyes framed by dark makeup, she tucked her straight, dyed-red hair behind one ear and revealed a line of piercings there too. Cal didn't say anything. Her voice didn't sound like the accents he'd heard in the city. Like him, she didn't seem native.

"Everybody clapping though? What the hell was that about? Like they're actually going to be happy!" She laughed, earning sighs of disapproval from the others in the elevator.

The way she said everybody, *Errybody*, made him smile.

"Hi," she said, "I'm Louise." The smile flashed at him, making him blush. "And y'all ain't from around here, are ya?"

"Cal," he muttered, "and no, what gave it away?" He tried to return the smile and suspected he may have crossed from awkward into creepy.

"Just a hunch," she said, one corner of her mouth curling up and making his heart skip a little.

They rode the rest of the way down in awkward silence, him trying to think of things to say to her, and her watching him with a smile of amusement at his discomfort. The doors opened and the elevator disgorged them all onto ground level. Cal walked slowly, hoping she would continue the conversation. He glanced behind him and saw that she had gone.

Shit, he thought, kicking himself for a wasted opportunity of some human contact to smother his sullen loneliness. Turning

55

back to the doors, he found himself staring into her amused face as she stood blocking his path.

"So, what are y'all fixin' to do now?" she asked him, the smile still there.

"Oh," Cal stammered, not understanding her use of her native vernacular, "it's just me actually …"

"I can see that, silly," Louise said. "Wanna grab a cup of coffee?"

Cal thought that sounded like a good idea. The best idea he'd heard in a long time actually. She indicated that he should follow her and set off at a brisk pace for the exit, forcing him to scurry to make up the lead she had extended. Cursing himself for falling in line so easily to chase another woman, he did the most British of things, and had a word with himself.

Play it cool, he thought, *or at least try to play it cool …*

They walked in silence for a while, Cal because he didn't know what to say and Louise because she evidently enjoyed a comfortable silence, even if it was only comfortable for her. She walked into the nearest coffee shop with its familiar green and white livery, bought herself a coffee with cream and two sugars, and stepped back for Cal to make his order as their barista, complete with his ironic moustache, wrote names on the paper cups.

"I'll have the same please, mate," he said to the vendor, feeling as though he'd made a mistake and Louise would think he was copying her.

"Funny," she said, "being from England and all, I thought you'd have tea."

Cal had never liked tea, had even refused it when it was the only hot drink—or brew as he would say—on offer when he desperately needed the comfort of one. He had even refused tea when he was offered a hot mug of it after finishing the last forced march, the final test to pass out as a Royal Marine so many years ago, even though he was frozen to the bone.

"Can't stand the stuff," he told her, earning another amused curling of her mouth. *Dammit,* he thought, *she's seriously cute. So why is she talking to me?*

Cal had been in a relationship with Angie for years, and had remained faithful throughout. When they ran out of things to talk about they moved in together, and when that exhausted their conversation points they—*she*—talked about getting married. Cal had taken the hints and bought an engagement ring, knowing her high expectations for what that ring should be like and how expensive it had to be. She'd said yes, and for the next year and a half he had saved and worked overtime to pay for the wedding. Her father had never approved of Cal, had told her that he wouldn't amount to anything because he lacked any vision of his future, and refused to pay for any part of it.

Working for a company which specialized in pouring concrete for mostly commercial buildings, Mr. Holt, the prospective father-in-law, had disapproved of him and his prospects, and had even once called him 'nothing but a lackey' to his face.

Cal didn't see it that way. He worked hard, and he had progressed as far as he could in that business, graduating to running projects on his own with laborers working under him. He had a company van which he could drive for personal use if he wanted to, and he was paid well enough. Since the engagement he had worked six, sometimes seven days a week and had offered to take the biggest jobs which involved the most travelling. He had almost doubled his usual wage in a few months, and every penny was saved for the wedding.

Which was all gone now, the only exception being the ridiculously expensive hotel room that was his for another few days and the flight home. The agreement was that Angie would save up for the spending money, which was why he was seeing the sights of New York City on a shoestring budget and still managing to max out his last credit card.

"So," Louise said, snapping his attention back to the present and out of his pit of self-absorbed misery as he followed her to a vacant booth to sit, "where y'all from exactly?"

58

"England," said Cal, not looking directly at her as he took a sip of the coffee, which was too hot to drink. Fighting the urge to react to his burning mouth he swallowed it, intensifying the pain and fighting his body not to show it in front of the woman who seemed not to think he was a waste of good air. She looked at him, her face saying, *well that much was obvious,* and he added a little more information to his answer.

"South of London," he said, trying to make his very boring hometown sound more interesting, "but I get into the city as much as I can." He had no idea why he added the last comment, a complete lie as he hated travelling into London and avoided it whenever he could. He supposed he was trying to make himself sound more metropolitan and interesting to her, and failing. Louise regarded him with another smile, head titled ever so slightly over as though she were gauging his responses.

"Should've come to the Empire State at dusk," she said, flipping the subject as though small talk was boring to her. "I've heard the views are much better when the sun's going down."

Cal struggled to find an appropriate response, anything which would make him sound smooth and mysterious, something James Bond would say. As the seconds ticked by and he realized he was just ignoring her, he clutched to the one part of her sentence he had picked up on.

"You've not been here before then?" he asked, his voice an octave higher than he thought it would be.

"Sweetie," she said sarcastically, tilting her head forwards as though she were looking over the rim of imaginary glasses, "does it sound like I'm one of them New Yorker types?"

Her calling him sweetie made the blood rush to his cheeks, and the resulting blush couldn't be hidden. It also served to, somehow, relax him and make him drop the façade of trying to sound like, and be, someone he wasn't. Cal laughed, as she had intended him to do, although with a little more nervous intensity than she expected.

"No," he said, "it doesn't. Are you from the South then?"

"Honey, you're in the northeast corner of the States," she said, "almost *errythang* is either south or west of here."

Another pet name, and a deeper blush from Cal.

"Your accent," he said, giving up, "where is it from?"

"Now you ask the right question!" she said, smiling. "I was born and raised in West Virginia."

"Ah," Cal said, taking a polite nibble of salted pretzel and a sip of coffee. Silence hung for a few seconds.

"Y'all have no idea where that is, do you?" she asked mockingly.

"Not a clue!" Cal answered, laughing with her.

"Well, Cal from England—south of London, what do you say we ditch the coffee and get ourselves a real drink?"

And, for the second time in an hour, Cal heard the best suggestion he'd heard in a long time.

TRY ANYTHING ONCE

Thursday 12:30 p.m. - Movement Headquarters

"T-minus twelve hours," the colonel rumbled to himself as he stood, hands on hips and feet squared apart as he scanned the news channels for any sign of things not going to plan.

"What are you looking for, Glenn?" asked Suzanne, safe in the knowledge he would allow her use of his first name as they were alone in the command center.

"Nothing. Anything," he answered enigmatically. "Any arrests for treason, any mention of the National Guard being stood down or under investigation. The president announcing a U-turn on defense cuts and standing down from office. Anything really," he said, explaining his fears as much as he would admit having any to anyone.

"Glenn," Suzanne began, but changed her approach when he turned to her looking all business again. "Sir," she said, "if I may?"

"Say what you want to say, Suzanne," the colonel replied almost testily, annoyed at himself for showing a crack in the armor.

"Sir, everything is in place. The pieces are on the board and they are set." She swallowed, drawing herself up and placing a hand on his shoulder, intuitively knowing that he was nervous. "You need to trust, Colonel. You need to trust your men, trust your lieutenants, trust *me*. Sir, with all due respect, will you just take a damned load off and try to relax for five minutes?"

Colonel Glenn Butler, unaccustomed to being spoken to by anyone like that, least of all a woman who wasn't his mother, smiled.

"Trust other people to do their duty? I've been trusting men to follow their orders and die for their country for forty years; *trust* isn't my issue here, but relax?" He paused, either unsure of how to say what he meant or unwilling to say it. "Relaxing is not something I know how to do," he finished.

"Well, sir, if I may," she said pulling open the door and inviting him outside. "Perhaps now is a good time to take a walk. Maybe you'll start there."

"Yes, ma'am. Try anything once," said Butler, doing as he was told and taking a walk.

Thursday 9:15 p.m. - Chelsea District, NYC

Cal returned from the bathroom to find that Louise had bought them another round. She was approaching her limit, a limit she knew well from too many mornings spent feeling ill and remembering the previous night one awful memory at a time.

She regarded herself as a free spirit; too easily bored to settle down and still so much of the world she needed to see. Everything amused her, even Cal giggling every time she said *errythang*, and she had enjoyed the city so far. Especially the weirdly hypnotic band playing South American music they saw in the subway on the way there, who had attracted a huge crowd and were selling their CDs right there. She had marveled at the panpipes and found herself almost entranced into staying and listening, as though they had cast some sort of spell over the commuters.

Not all of the city was to her liking though. She found many of the people to be brash and, like city dwellers all over the country, very few of them had time for someone from out of town unless they were getting paid to talk to them. The city was as far away from her upbringing as she could get, even though the distance wasn't that great—under six hundred miles—which to Cal was huge but then again, she doubted if he had grasped the size of the country he was in.

She doubted if anyone in the bar had ever been horseback riding, or deer hunting. She pitied these urban types, as she called them, whereas others from her hometown, which was little more than a speck on the map nestled between Highway 77 and the Ohio river, envied them.

"Where are you staying?" Cal asked her, far more relaxed and talkative now that three beers and four tequilas had loosened his awkwardness.

"Oh, some dive," Louise responded with a wave of her hand, throwing back her drink and grimacing before her face cracked back into a smile. "There's a shared bathroom!"

"Hang on," said Cal, "there's not even a toilet in the room?"

She laughed, and repeated the unfamiliar and very British word back to him. Her pronunciation of the word toilet made Cal erupt into more laughter.

"What I say now?" Louise said with mock indignation. "You keep laughin' about how I talk, when you should hear yourself!"

"I'm sorry," Cal said, spluttering, "I just have no idea how you managed to put an 'R' in the word toilet!"

"It's true though!" Louise went on, enjoying herself. "I took one look at that sink and I said to myself, 'Darlin', you don't want to use that sink with how far away the *toilet* is' if you catch my meanin'?"

Cal did, and he thought this was hilarious not just because she had turned her accent all the way up to eleven to tell him the story, but because she'd said the word toilet again. He stopped laughing as she settled back to lean on the table and tucked her hair behind her ear again. By joint agreement, the atmosphere seemed to change.

"So," she said, "y'all going to explain why you're out here all by your lonesome?"

The elephant in the room had been addressed. It was clear to Cal that Louise was one of those free-spirit types who could just set off for somewhere new at a moment's notice, but it was obvious to anyone that Cal wasn't alone by choice.

"I'm here on my honeymoon," Cal announced, raising his glass to her and knocking back the drink. Louise's face froze, trying to work out if he was serious or not, and hoping that she hadn't just wasted hours talking to a married man—she couldn't abide cheating, having seen first-hand the damage it does to people. Cal saw the look on her face and tried to recover.

"But I'm on my own because the wedding never happened," he told her.

Louise seemed to perk up at this, but still wasn't sure.

"She walked out on me, five bloody days before the wedding, with my best friend," he said, the sullen anger returning to his eyes as they watered involuntarily. "They're probably in my house right now, and you know the best thing?" He paused, making her uncertain whether the question was rhetorical or not. "She wanted to come on the trip and bring him instead!" His anger surged again but he managed to keep it inside as he remembered the text he got asking to buy his ticket from him. He had politely, yet firmly, told her to go fuck herself. His hand twitched toward his pocket, but the part of him that was still sober stopped the movement. Bringing out the little box now would guarantee to scare her off.

"Oh," Louise said, lost for words for the first time in as long as she could recall. "I just thought you'd argued with your friends or something …"

"Nope," Cal said, the momentary anger being forced away as he tried to make himself sound jovial again. "Here on my own, seeing the sights, and enjoying all the money I've saved up for over a year to put her up in the bloody Waldorf because she *had* to stay there."

Louise, despite the high levels of ambient noise, let out a low whistle, which penetrated the din and brought Cal's smile back.

"*The* Waldorf?" she said incredulously, leaning forward. "I can't even afford to park my car near there." She paused, thinking. "Heck, I can't even afford a car!"

They both laughed, but Louise was clearly impressed. It wasn't like he was one of those rich people that Sebastian knew by name, he was just a fool who had worked hard and saved up to impress a girl, but the girl who was impressed wasn't the one he originally intended. He was okay with that.

"My hotel is like, thirty bucks a night and I swear to god, I take the stairs every time to the fourth floor because I think that elevator might just fall down much as I even look at it!"

Cal laughed again. Her manner, the way she spoke, the way she entertained him with a story when she could've offered a boring but short answer, intoxicated him. The alcohol intoxicated him too, but he just couldn't get enough of her because she was so unlike any woman he'd ever spoken to. She had literally nothing in common with Angie except her species and gender, and even Cal had begun to doubt Angie's membership of the human race recently.

"So anyway," he said, "now that's out in the open, what about you?"

"Me?" said Louise, hand on her chest as though he had accused her of something. "Well I'm just an open book."

"No," Cal said laughing, "you're not!"

"Well," Louise replied, "if y'all want to get all deep and meaningful, I'm gonna need some more drinks."

Louise was aware that she was spending more than she had meant to that day, and each day of her trip had a strict cash allowance that had to be kept to or she would have to go home sooner. She had worked as a waitress for months, spending as little as she could, getting by and waiting for the day she could escape again for somewhere different. She had done this a dozen times; saved up and gone on an adventure before having to come back and beg for her job back. She got it back every time, and the owner of the diner just accepted that it was what Louise did. Her feet just didn't want to stay still.

Truth was that she did have somewhere to be, but she felt trapped by the open air and the same sidewalks under her shoes every single day. As soon as she was back, as soon as she had lied to everyone about how good it was to be home, she was already thinking about where to head next. She would stick her finger on the map of the United States, and she would go there. Six months ago, she had heard someone in the diner talking about their trip to New York City, and about how much they hated it there with the smog and the tourists and the cops on every corner, but Louise had listened and decided that maybe she needed to see that city for herself.

To hell with it, she thought, buying two more beers and two chasers to go with them. *If I have to go home a day early to spend tonight getting an Englishman drunk, then god dammit I will.*

"So, what have you seen in this fine city, Cal?" she said as she returned to their table with the four glasses held expertly in both hands.

"Rockefeller building," Cal said, after sketching a 'cheers' and taking a pull of beer. "It looked big and busy so I didn't go in."

"Well, ain't y'all the fearless tourist?" Louise said, laughing at him.

"And I went to Central Park and saw the zoo," he added.

"Saw it or went inside and saw it?" Louise shot back, drinking her beer but keeping her eyes on him.

"I actually went inside," he said, sounding proud of himself, "and I went on an uncomfortable boat around some big statue thing with a hangover, saw someone playing saxophone in the subway, had a snake draped around my neck, then went up the Empire State building where I saw a man throw his life away."

They both laughed, both having the same feelings about the proposal. She called it lame whereas Cal said it was cheesy.

"And met a delightful young redhead who then led you astray into a night of ungodly depravity?" she finished for him.

Picking up the chaser in the smaller glass, he raised it to her and said, "Here's hoping!"

Throwing back her drink in a movement identical to Cal's, she smiled at him playfully.

"Always wanted to see the inside of a fancy hotel room."

Thursday 10:28 p.m. - Wall Street

The dull gray van nosed sedately through the late evening traffic, pulling into a manned security gate. The uniformed guard put on his hat, picked up the clipboard with the day's schedule on, and left his small booth to speak to the driver.

"Hey Gerry. Hey Siobhan," the guard said, greeting the overnight cleaning crew who worked Wednesday through Friday.

70

"Hey Simon," replied Gerry, the balding middle-aged driver, "busy night?"

"Ah, you know," Simon answered casually, "another day …"

"Ain't that the truth!" called Siobhan from the passenger side.

Simon checked them off the list on his clipboard, as he had done most weeks for a year, and didn't bother searching the van as he was supposed to. There was no point, he told himself, eager to get back to his seat to carry on with the book he was reading. It was just cleaning products like always. He only searched them when someone else was around anyway, just for show, and the new supervisor never bothered reviewing the overnight camera footage like the last guy did.

Once inside the gates and through the metal roller shutter Simon had opened from inside his booth, Gerry nodded once to his wife. Silently, they got their equipment from the sliding door on the side of the van and both lifted the heavy trolley to the ground; heavy because wrapped in black plastic sacks and covered by the rest of their cleaning products was the last invention of one Quentin Aaronson. Taking it to the basement where it was tucked inside a large waste bin next to the banks of flickering lights in the air-conditioned section to keep the computers running at optimal temperature, Siobhan peeled back the heavy plastic and checked her watch. She set the timer on the device, replaced the cover and nodded again to her husband.

These computer things, whatever they were and not that she cared, were checked and maintained every Monday night and the device would be safe from prying eyes until the timer expired.

Without another word, they went back upstairs and cleaned the offices as they always had.

Above ground outside, Simon leaned back and tipped his hat up a little as he licked his thumb and turned the page of his book in total ignorance as to what his apathy had just allowed.

Thursday 11.46 p.m. - Floyd Bennet Field, Brooklyn

The routine maintenance of the NYPD's helicopters was a constant task, operating day and night. Gus Daly, a wizened old man who had been servicing helicopters for longer than he could recall, scanned the lines of the NYPD's air support choppers. The four Bell 412 medium lifts and the smaller, more tactical, Bell 429s were his babies as he called them, and it tore his heart to do what he was about to.

Still the money was good—too good to say no—and he also strongly suspected that saying no wasn't an option to the guys who had found him at his favorite bar.

Almost all of the aircraft were on the tarmac, with only two on a call and one inside the hangar for a repair. Nobody would think anything of Gus wandering between the helicopters parked up, running a hand along the fuselage almost tenderly, checking his babies over. He fitted each one with a small device, cell phones taped to their exteriors, tucking them away where they couldn't be discovered by chance. Regretting his decision to conspire with the men, he still couldn't bring himself to change his mind because he needed that money.

"You promise me they won't be damaged? And no one will get hurt?" he had asked the frightening men with the bag of cash and the bag of devices.

"Nobody will be hurt," lied the first man, the only one who spoke.

Gus accepted that, because the money had blinded him to the subtext of their conversation. It seemed to Gus that patriotism and loyalty, like everything in life, had a price.

PLANNING THE EXECUTION, EXECUTING THE PLAN

Friday 8:30 a.m. - Waldorf Astoria, NYC

Cal woke with the events of the previous night flooding back to him. With a nervous intensity, his eyes slowly moved to his right where the smooth skin of Louise's bare back rose and fell gently with each breath. He held his gaze on her back for a while, studying the tattoo on her shoulder.

Creeping out of bed as quietly as he could, he tiptoed to the bathroom where he ran the shower to cover the noise of emptying his bladder after a night of drinking. He didn't feel hungover, most likely because their night had only ended a matter of a few hours ago and he was probably still a little drunk. As he let the hot water flow down his body, he stiffened in sudden fright as a pair of hands snaked around him. Wordlessly, he turned to face her as she moved closer under the water.

After their long shower together and the resulting activity leaving the hotel room looking like it had been wrecked, Cal led Louise down the elevator and the two sat eating breakfast, stealing shy smiles at one another.

"What do you want to do today?" Cal asked her expectantly.

"I promised a friend I'd catch up with her," she replied smiling, bursting his bubble that the free-spirited woman would be his for another day.

"Oh, I …" Cal trailed away, not knowing how to ask her if she wanted to spend more time with him. She intercepted his failing good mood.

"Wanna meet up again later?" she asked, making his spirits soar back to their original height and keep climbing.

"Yes!" Cal replied, too loud and too quickly. "I mean, yes, please. If you don't mind?"

Laughing at his eagerness and awkwardness, she smiled at him before speaking through half a mouthful of pancakes.

"Of course I don't mind, silly," she said. "Shall I come back here or do you want to come to my place?" The playful smile said it all. After her descriptions about how bad her hotel was, the answer was obvious.

"Let's stay at my place, shall we?" Cal replied with an attempted American accent.

"Yes please," she said, attempting her own approximation of Cal's accent and managing to make the conversation sound like a low-budget production of *Mary Poppins*, "if you don't mind?"

"Not at all," he said, blushing with excitement and happiness.

They agreed a time to meet, and he got an additional key card from the reception desk which he insisted she take despite her saying that it was too much. He told her if she got back first to grab a shower and order a bottle of something from room service, thinking that the cost would be worth it for her company.

"What are y'all doing this morning then?" she asked him, stacking up more pancakes and impaling them on her fork.

"No idea," he replied honestly, "where would you suggest?"

"Well that depends," she answered seriously, pausing to chew as she pointed the fork at him, "do the tourist thing, or go and see the real power of the US and visit the stock exchange!"

"Okay!" said Cal, calling her bluff and taking the suggestion seriously.

~

Riding the subway and wearing a stupid smile of satisfaction and happiness, Cal headed south and rose above ground to the packed streets around Wall Street. He felt as though he were intruding in the busy seat of western capitalism, as though every man or woman wearing a suit and walking fast with their eyes glued to their cell phones were a millionaire investment banker he associated with movies he had seen.

Wandering carefree through the streets, which yesterday had caused him to feel lonely and oppressed, he smiled at everything he saw. Turning into the street under guidance from the map on his phone, he saw military personnel patrolling in pairs, heavy barriers erected to prevent cars from entering the street, and no less than six officers of the NYPD visible in the iconic uniform which was such an everyday sight for native New Yorkers, but a tourist attraction in itself for Cal.

Craning his head back a little, he paused amidst the rushing crowds to take a picture of the Stock Exchange.

Friday 12:25 p.m. - Free America Movement Headquarters

"Butler," he said into the phone after the room had been cleared of all personnel. "Yes, confirm we are good to go," he said, hanging up the phone and calling his staff back inside where they had all congregated to watch the news screens.

~

On the other end of the satellite call, the voice signing off from Butler put down their equivalent device and picked up the landline on the desk. Speaking rapidly in English but using a complex series of words, which made no sense to anyone overhearing the one-sided conversation, he replaced the handset and leaned back in satisfaction.

Saturday 12:25 a.m. Local Time, Beijing

Sixty-six hundred miles away, another man had received a phone call. After listening intently to the information, he replaced the handset and leaned back to look up into the expectant faces of a half-dozen uniformed officers and one mysterious woman in a dark suit. The intelligence services wore no rank or insignia, and offered no names—only their department. That opened any door, and removed all but the most secure of resistance to their questions.

Speaking rapidly but strongly in Mandarin, he gave a short speech and issued orders.

"The operation is about to proceed as planned," he said, feeling the nervous tension in the room. "To your duties," he ordered, and the office emptied leaving only a black-suited woman. She approached the man at the desk, intimidating him with her sheer presence.

"You are sure of this?" she asked, the threat of failure evident in her tone.

"Yes," he replied, meeting her gaze as though he truly believed his answer. "By tomorrow we will have crippled them and their eyes will be facing elsewhere," he said, showing her a clenched fist to emphasize his point.

Friday 12:28 p.m. – Washington, D.C.

"Atteeeeen-HUH," called the master sergeant. Major Taylor walked into the hangar-sized building flanked by his junior officers to the sound of his brigade stamping their boots.

"At ease," he called out, removing his cap and surveying the front rank of his troops decked out in full battle gear.

"You know what we are doing here will be called treason by some," he said, as though everyone present didn't realize the danger of the mission. "Anyone wishing to stand down has my permission to do so now. You will not be punished, but you will be confined to barracks under guard until the mission is complete." He let that hang, watching his assembled force for any sign of hesitation.

Every man and woman, every soldier under his command, stared resolutely forward. He took that as a sign that nobody had second thoughts.

"Okay then. Team one is under the command of Captain Anderson, the rest are with me as QRF. Let's move out!"

Taylor replaced his cap and turned to the passenger side of the command Humvee. His battle helmet was on the seat and he switched the cap for the ballistic protection. Dressed similarly to his troops, including the M4 propped against the seat, his decision to lead the quick reaction force gave him an element of removal from the mission which gave him better oversight. He trusted Anderson to do his duty, and the hand-picked members of team one had his total faith. The big engine gunned and rolled out, followed by the second Humvee and the three troop carriers behind.

~

Rodriguez halted his truck just inside the entrance to the Holland tunnel and hit the four-way flashers. He checked his watch, closed the door of the cab and walked away. A dozen other small trucks were doing the same all over the city, and each stranded vehicle, one by one, caught fire from the incendiary device buried in the load of waste PVC plastic. Within minutes, almost every major route in and out of the city was a panicked mess of boiling black smoke and toxic fumes.

~

Leland checked his watch and held his breath as the seconds ticked down. His watch was analogue, a relic he had to wind up daily, but it kept good time and wouldn't be affected by what was about to happen. Glancing up at the skyline of Wall Street, he muttered a single word to himself.

"Go."

ORDO AB CHAO

Friday 12:30 p.m. - New York Stock Exchange

At the precise moment it was supposed to, the timer attached to the suitcase-sized EMP buried deep in the bowels of the exchange ticked to zero, and a loud click echoed amongst the whirring banks of flashing lights. A strange hum reverberated through the air, almost imperceptibly, and the banks of computers went dark all at once.

Upstairs on the trading floor, where sweat-covered men and women shouted to one another with phones pressed to their ears, the lights went out. The computers stopped working and blinked into oblivion, and the noise first rose in intensity to a deafening crescendo, then fell to a grumbling as they all waited for the backup power to come online and reboot the world market.

Seconds ticked by and nothing happened. Voices began to rise to demand the power come back on, as though rude indignation and the feeling that time was money could will it to happen. Still nothing happened.

The collective intelligence of everyone on the floor failed to grasp that their machines were not going to come back to life, and they milled about in confusion like chickens in a coop waiting to be fed.

A muted crack and an answering rumble penetrated the sounds inside the building, causing a moment of silence before shouted questions began to pierce the grumbling.

~

Outside, just as Cal was trying to get the right angle for his selfie, the screen of his phone unexpectedly went black. Frowning, he tried to turn it back on without success. He cursed the phone, the manufacturers, and everything else as he had just seen the battery indicator showing 88 percent before it died. Reverting to the most British of approaches when dealing with faulty technology, he tried to hit it twice and turn it on again without success.

Just as he was coming to terms that he was now in the dark ages and cut off from the world he accessed through the phone, he glanced around to see almost everyone else doing the same.

Hang on, he thought, *that can't be right.*

Just as the realization hit home that something had affected the entire area and not singled him out to ruin his day, a loud crack rang out from a nearby street.

He couldn't have known, but a trash can had exploded on the street, killing six pedestrians outright and blowing out the plate glass windows of all the nearby stores in great shards. Smoke rose from the explosion and caused instant panic.

Cal had ducked instinctively at the sudden noise, not having heard anything similar for many years but never forgetting the sound. As vivid as his distant memory was when it came to explosions and war, the city of New York had a far more intense collective memory when it came to terror attacks.

Fearing the reactions of the people more than the explosion, Cal turned and began walking fast in the opposite direction, desperate to get off the street as a second sound reached his ears. The unmistakable whoosh of a rocket and the answering crack of a second explosion ripped the air.

It was definitely time to get the hell out of there.

~

A woman with her hoodie pulled up hiding her face in shadow skipped down the steps of the subway station, her backpack bouncing uncomfortably as its heavy load impacted her lower back. Slipping it from her shoulders, she flicked a switch on the top and surreptitiously dropped it at the side of a trash can. The subway was so busy, and everyone but the crazies avoided eye contact, so it was a simple thing to do and remain unnoticed. Jumping through the sliding doors of the train about to depart, she flicked back her hood and checked her watch.

~

Captain Michael Anderson led his troops along Washington Avenue and right up to the gates of the power plant.

"Sir, you need to evacuate this facility immediately," he barked at the guard on the gate, brandishing a blank sheet of paper as though it were his authority to demand action.

Act like you own the place, his father had once told him before he left home to join the military, *and remember it's only you who will know that you don't have the authority.*

So now he did just that, and all his bluster, urgency and authority terrified the guard. He didn't know what to do first, but before he could even formulate any answer Anderson snapped at him again.

"Get this goddamned gate open, now, and clear the area!" he yelled, climbing back into the Humvee. The gate slid open, and Anderson's vehicle led the way inside at speed leaving a stunned guard totally unsure what to do next. He decided that the best course of action was to hit the alarm button, and evacuate the area immediately, just as he was told to.

By the time Anderson's convoy had arrived at the main plant, people were already starting to file out of the entrance in confusion. He had to maintain his momentum, not allow time or opportunity for anyone to question his presence there or that of thirty heavily armed National Guardsmen. Yelling at the workers to evacuate, he pushed inside. His troops followed, repeating his orders for people to get the fuck out of there and ad-libbing with pushes and curses as the confused workers sped up for the exits.

An audible alarm was sounding now, adding to the panic and making it easier to get everyone out. Their intelligence said that less than a hundred civilians would be on site, and that seemed consistent with the exodus Anderson was witnessing.

Halting, taking a knee and pulling out a schematic drawing, he glanced around and pointed toward a tall structure. No orders were necessary; the four-man team carrying a heavy load between them trotted toward it. The device had been collected in secret that morning, a tired courier giving the instruction face-to-face from memory, and to his eyes was more than big enough to perform the task. His two trained EOD—explosive ordnance disposal—guys set it up and gave him a thumbs-up sign.

"Two-minute warning, clear out," he yelled, seeing his troops scurrying for the exit. Last man out, Anderson stole a last glance at the device from the threshold and saw a man in the uniform of the plant leaning over it and pulling a call phone from his pocket.

Anderson dropped to one knee again and raised his rifle. The man filled the optic, meaning that he couldn't miss from that distance, and he didn't hesitate. Firing two short bursts, Anderson reacquired the target to see the man slumped lifelessly over the device. He sensed two of his soldiers returning to offer him fire support, knowing that both would be scanning for a target which had caused their officer to fire his weapon.

"Move out," he said, climbing back to his feet, and setting off for the Humvee at a run.

His troops were bawling at the crowd of workers to get back, to clear the area, as some had returned to find out the source of the obvious gunfire. Bypassing the vehicles, he ran to the front and pushed through the line of soldiers. Without hesitation once more, he flicked the safety off his weapon and emptied the remainder of the magazine into the air.

"Get the fuck back!" he screamed at them. "The plant is going to blow!"

This got their attention, and they turned and ran. The speed at which they were running in obvious desperation made Anderson worry about the blast radius. He climbed back into the vehicle and led the convoy back to Washington Avenue, his driver weaving around the fleeing workers expertly before he was forced to slow at the gate. Anderson was watching in the side mirror as the sudden crunch of tires jolted him forwards. Turning to his driver he saw the young man's eyes locked ahead, just as he turned his head to see three Metro police cruisers slew to block the road. Five cops got out of the three cars and took cover behind the engine blocks, all aiming their sidearms at the lead Humvee.

Anderson was no coward. He regretted having to kill the man in the plant but his use of a cell phone next to an armed explosive device was a risk he couldn't allow, as a premature detonation could endanger the lives of his men. Still, engaging local police in a one-sided gunfight was not a prospect he relished; these cops were like him, just troops doing their jobs.

The decision to engage was taken out of his hands.

Taylor's QRF had been on approach when the cruisers pulled up. Without hesitation, and perhaps more bloodthirsty than Anderson, he ordered his driver to take them out. Their Humvee hit the first cruiser side-on, crushing it into the second car and the two cops taking cover between the cars with it. The two wrecks piled into the third, ramming it up the curb and flipping it onto its side where it landed on another cop and killed him instantly.

With the road clear, Anderson's convoy fell in line behind Taylor's as they headed for Capitol Hill. Behind them, the air turned bright red and then went black as the huge explosion ripped the power plant to pieces, shutting down the power grid to the whole city.

~

Cal regained his feet from the horror of the explosion at the subway after the backpack's contents had incinerated the stairwell. His confusion and fear were running at previously unknown levels, but he needed the safety and security of somewhere away from this place of fire and screams. Something in his subconscious told him to start running, to get back to the hotel, and be safe. He had run almost an entire block north, at least he hoped it was north, before it dawned on him that Louise was out there somewhere. He hadn't even asked which part of the city she was visiting, eager not to cramp her free-spirited style with such mundane questions.

He fled, breathing heavily as the deafness became a painful screeching in his skull as muted sounds returned to him. He could make out screams, and even more sirens than normal. Everywhere people ran, desperate to find safety but not knowing where to get it.

Twice more he was knocked to the ground by panicked people running and not looking where they were going as the mass of bodies sought refuge off the streets. Buildings were being assaulted by crowds trying to get under cover but still Cal ran as best he could to get back to his hotel, to find Louise, and to get the hell out of there.

Traffic was at a total standstill, and when Cal got out to the bigger streets he saw vehicles being abandoned where they sat in the traffic jams with people leaving their doors open and running. A woman was trying to get the seatbelt off her terrified daughter and almost dragged the girl from the car to sweep her up into her arms. She paused, the child screaming and crying next to her ear, to lock her car with the key fob and zip her purse closed before she hefted the girl higher and ran with her left hand protectively over the back of the child's head. Everywhere Cal looked, he saw people in need of help. People surged in and out of the subway entrances, not knowing what he knew about the explosion which could have killed him, but his shouts of warning went unheard.

Prioritize, he thought sternly, *look after yourself.*

Even in his current state of physical fitness, five miles would have been an easy distance to cover. Five miles over broken ground without the added incentive of staying alive would have been easier than what he faced, as five miles across a packed city where panic and chaos spread like tear gas was almost impossible. He ran so hard that he even escaped some of the terror for a time, until the news of what had happened spread further up the island.

Cal didn't know, but the island of Manhattan was effectively cut off and things were only going to get worse.

THE VALUE OF SUCCESS

Colonel Butler stood at the front of his assembled command center staff with Suzanne at his side. He watched the bank of screens, scanning the ticker-tape text scrolling from right to left for information and occasionally calling out to an aide to record something.

One screen showed an image of black smoke pouring from a tunnel entrance, and a reporter holding a microphone, scanning her eyes left and right as she nervously gave the report, obviously wanted to get out of there.

"Holland tunnel," Butler said, snapping his fingers, and pointing at a young man with a clipboard. The man hurriedly searched for the mission objective on his list and ticked it off. Butler was happy, because he was winning. Another screen showed an aerial view from a helicopter filming the devastation in Washington where the power plant had previously been. Now it was a smoking crater, betraying a blast radius far bigger than their estimates imagined, and he watched as the footage switched to blackened and destroyed police cars thrown hundreds of yards away. The footer on the screen showed the evocative title:

"Terror Attack on Capitol Hill"

He said a silent prayer of thanks to Taylor, seeing the success and dedication his team had showed, and wished him well in his next mission.

Turning his eyes back to the footage from New York, some of it obviously taken from cell phone videos uploaded to the internet, he saw different pillars of smoke rising from the subway stations and streets. Leland had done well, but there was yet to be any mention of the stock exchange being permanently shut down. No doubt the eyes of the city were on the series of small explosions and fires instead of their investment portfolios. The attack on New York City had gone well, very well, and even now the city-wide panic began to breed and grow at an unfathomable rate. The idea was not to destroy the city but to cause widespread fear and chaos, which it seemed was happening as he watched. Already the news reported looting happening in parts of the city which were unaffected by the bombs.

"Are we ready for phase three?" Suzanne asked him.

"Not yet," Butler replied. His eyes never stopping scanning the screens for a second, as he assimilated so many different sources of information but still remained present in the room. "We're waiting for the response before we show that card. We wait."

Suzanne nodded, not that he saw her gesture, and lapsed back into silence as she too watched the screens.

"That's Willis Avenue Bridge," she said, recognizing the scene from another news channel, and the bearer of another clipboard searched their list to record it.

The title from the news channel showing events in Washington changed then, the text reading "No response from the White House," and showed military vehicles at the iconic building. Muzzle flashes sparkled brightly on the screen, catching Butler's eye.

"Turn up the sound on screen four," he called to the room, rightly expecting that someone would obey his order and not make him wait. Within a second the graphic showed up on the bottom of the screen and the numbers blurred as the volume went high.

"...*what appears to be gunfire on the White House lawn. The National Guard are on site and seem to be engaged in a firefight with unknown gunmen inside the grounds ...*"

The reporter giving the commentary clearly had not the first clue about a firefight. If anyone had looked at the big picture there, it would be obvious to them that the National Guard were moving forwards in a well-drilled tactical formation, firing and maneuvering as other squads provided covering fire, and were assaulting the building. The people the news anchor had called 'unknown gunmen' were the Secret Service responding to the threat of attack.

Butler, having been involved in and commanding more fire-fights than he cared to remember, appreciated the discipline of the troops. The Secret Service, as well trained and incredibly well equipped as they were, did not have the odds on their side as a brigade of battle-ready troops stormed their gates appearing to be friendly. The 9mm rounds coming from their service-issued weapons, the only firearms available to them at immediate notice, embedded in the ballistic vests of the troops they were lucky or skilled enough to hit. In contrast, firing full-auto 5.56 ammunition and working in effective fire teams, the troops overwhelmed them in minutes as Butler and his team watched. Stacking up to breach the doors and filing inside to perform a brutal room clearance, Butler saw a glimpse of the man leading them and knew his message had been received five by five.

Taylor was making it happen.

"Sir!" someone said in a shrill voice which bordered on pan-ic, annoying the colonel with the tone of lapsed discipline.

"What?" he growled in response, to see the same young man with his clipboard pointing at another screen. Snatching up two remotes as he dropped the clipboard, the man simultaneously muted the Washington news screen and raised the volume of another. This one showed an airstrip, with two F-35s blasting away into the sky. Butler didn't need any screen text to know that the Naval Airbase in Virginia had responded to the perceived terrorist threat in New York City.

This was expected, and catered for. As much as the American people didn't like to admit it, the military response post 9-11 was swift and under brutally strict orders. Anything in the air which did not respond to their hails to break away from the air space would be assumed to be under terrorist control. It was an uncomfortable truth, but the reality was that these Naval aviators were there to shoot down anything potentially unfriendly in the skies.

"Prepare to start phase three," he said calmly, despite the obvious fear of a military response some of his team were radiating. He turned to face them.

"Those jets aren't coming here, they're heading for New York. We've anticipated this and planned for it, so you carry on with your job, son, and leave those aircraft to me." He turned back to the screens as Suzanne rejoined him, holding out a burner phone. It had been tested once, using a different phone on the same network, so he knew the signal would go out. Turning it on he took a piece of paper from Suzanne, input the different cell numbers into the message recipient field, and handed the phone and paper back to Suzanne to be double-checked. She read each one carefully and handed it back.

"Good to go, sir," she said.

"Outstanding," Butler said loudly, exuding the confidence of a leader who knows some of his troops are experiencing the fear of conflict for the first time.

"I expect those fighter planes to be approaching the city within ten minutes"—he checked his watch— "so phase three will begin at 13:07 local time."

With that, he smiled and turned his attention back to the screens, keeping a careful eye on the Washington news channel.

~

Seven thousand miles away as the crow flies, if a crow could traverse half the earth, at one in the morning was a similar command center. This one, as with any modern tactical command hub, did bristle with wires and phone lines. Banks of screens showed live news from all around the world, and a digital bank of clocks gave local time for every major city in the world.

This part of the operation was critical, as so many factors could be controlled with the exception of foreign interference beyond their influence.

The woman in the dark suit watched with her cold expression giving nothing away; she could be angry or she could be experiencing the happiest moment of her life, only nobody but her would know. She watched as the flaming jet trails of the two

F-35s soared away from the ground and the camera shot panned out to see the aircraft disappearing over a fluttering stars and stripes flag.

Internally she sneered as her face remained as stone. Their theatrical sense of national pride would soon suffer irreparably, she reminded herself.

FALLING SKIES

Cal was making slower progress now, as the streets became packed with people fleeing the financial district. Some had been sensible and had headed south for the ferries which would revert to evacuation at the first sign of any attack, but even if he had thought of it, that wasn't an option for Cal. His passport was in his hotel room safe, but the biggest priority was to find the only person on this island he cared about.

In contrast to the chaos and panic in the streets, he saw a table of five people a little younger than himself inside a coffee shop. They were sat in silence, but all were still and calm as they sipped their drinks from oversized cups. Shaking away the image of them, to Cal the image of stupidity and a lack of any sense of self-preservation, he jolted back to the present with a painful impact.

A cab driver had decided to ignore the rules of the one-way streets, and broke free from the traffic jam by clipping the bumper of the car in front and spinning his tires as he shot down a side street against the normal flow of traffic. He did this at the exact moment Cal ran into the road.

Rolling up the windshield and hitting his lower back sharply on the taxi sign on the roof, the cab stopped and rolled him back down over the hood to slam into the street again. Groaning in agony and shock as he took a long, tortured breath to fill his lungs, Cal rose unsteadily to his feet and limped to the passenger side of the vehicle where his confusion made him instinctively think the driver would be sitting behind the wheel there. He wasn't entirely sure what he wanted to say to the cabbie, other than to give him abuse, but he never got the opportunity as the tires screeched again and the cab took off down the street.

"PRICK!" Cal shouted after him impotently.

"Hey, buddy. You okay?" said a voice behind him, still muted by the temporary deafness he suffered. Cal turned to see a man, olive skinned and dark haired in appearance with the contrasting twang in his voice of a New Yorker. He had his sleeves rolled up and wore a grease-splattered apron which Cal imagined had been white at one point in its existence.

"You got yourself hit pretty good there, huh guy?" he said, his face showing a mixture of concern and amusement.

"Yeah," groaned Cal, bending at the waist to try and catch his breath as he screwed his eyes shut. "Fucking arsehole," he said, meaning the cab driver.

"Buddy, listen, forget about it. The whole city's going nuts out here and you need to get yourself someplace safe, huh?" the man said, eyes darting around at the rising panic.

"You too," said Cal, standing up stiffly. He knew that he was going to be in some serious pain tomorrow.

"Oh, I will, don't you worry," he replied with a chuckle. "But I need to lock up my deli first so none of these dumb schmucks decide to do a little redecorating. After that I'm checking out if you know what I mean?"

"Yeah," said Cal again as he wavered on the spot with a wave of dizziness.

"Buddy, you don't look so good …" the deli owner said, eyeing the Brit with concern.

"I need to get to the Waldorf," Cal told him, his desperate need coming back to him, "which way do I go?"

His concern forgotten, and the chaos enveloping the city momentarily pushed aside, the man launched into directions. "Okay, what you want to do is head north on 3rd, take a left on 23rd for two blocks then head north on Park." The man glanced side to side and bounced his shoulders as he talked.

"Thanks," Cal grunted through gritted teeth before he straightened up and went to walk away.

"Buddy, that's west! You gotta get your bearings," he was told, but any further response was drowned out by a helicopter coming in low.

~

The pilot of the Bell 429 came in low and slow, heading toward the financial district after they were re-tasked from monitoring the vehicle fires on Broadway. As they passed overhead, never knowing about the conversation between a British man who just lost a fight with a city cab and a local shopkeeper, a text message was received onboard.

The cell phone taped securely to the small box hidden away toward the back of the cabin lit up, connected the circuitry inside, and blinked out.

Simultaneously, the instrumentation onboard also blacked out, and as the pilot fought to control the flightless bird he suddenly found himself in, gravity did what it did best, and reminded the human race that they had never evolved to fly.

~

"Abort! Abort!" shouted the F-35 pilot as he yanked the stick toward him, put the machine at a right angle to the earth, and punched it. Climbing straight up at hundreds of miles per hour, his wing man copied the maneuver instinctively. Hitting the radio mic, he hailed Chambers Field.

"C-F, C-F, this is Phantom. Be advised we are bugging out. NYPD rotary wings have been downed by unknown E-W. Repeat, NYPD birds have been downed by E-W," he reported, his voice muffled and robotic partially disguising a Florida accent.

"Say again, Phantom," came the reply from the Chambers Field naval airbase in Virginia.

"I say again C-F," the pilot said in a voice which made it clear he wasn't impressed with the request. Reducing his airspeed and rolling to level out and point the nose of his aircraft toward home with the blood returning to the front half of his body, he said, "Unknown electronic warfare in play. NYPD rotary wings are down. I saw two drop simultaneously. We are not equipped with ECM and request orders to RTB. Repeat, we are not equipped with ECM and have no response to threat."

A pause before the radio operator came back.

Phantom imagined the base commander standing behind her, the handset of a landline pressed to his shoulder with an important call waiting. The F-35 truly was at the cutting edge of fighter plane technology; its onboard computer systems were capable of identifying threats and deploying countermeasures in an instant without the need for the human pilot to react. What Phantom had seen, however, was what he truly believed was a directed energy weapon or something similar, and he didn't much like the thought of having his ride go dark on him.

"Negative on the RTB, Phantom," said the voice in his ear. "Climb to ninety-eight hundred feet and stay on target as CAP.

Repeat, floor of operations is now ninety-eight hundred. Acknowledge," she ordered.

"C-F, Phantom. Acknowledged."

The lead F-35 banked hard left, sweeping around to return to Manhattan, only this time climbing to a much higher altitude. It could only have been some kind of EMP or energy weapon that could cause the two helicopters he saw to both go dark and drop in perfect synchronicity, but now any directed electronic warfare weaponry would have to be flying alongside them at a little over two hundred and fifty miles an hour to take them down.

This way they were still on site to conduct their primary role, that of a combat air patrol, but the new floor of operation being raised to the three-kilometer mark made them, in theory, safe from the threat without electronic jamming countermeasures. Height advantage or not, both pilots were very nervous at the prospect of having their fifty-million-dollar plane's electronics fried with them in the driving seats.

~

Cal woke, coughing and spluttering, with an incredible pain in his head.

"Hey, buddy. You okay?" came the familiar voice. Cal was confused, thinking that when he got hit with the car he hadn't actually got up, and had some weird dream or premonition. His eyes saw ceiling, and his brain registered that he was now inside instead of on the street.

Cal saw the man who asked him again if he was okay, and squinted as he looked around the dark room. Sound from outside penetrated his thoughts and he registered a lot more screaming and sirens than previously.

"What happened?" he asked, realizing that the deli owner's apron now sported a bright, wet bloodstain over the patterns of grease.

"Heck do I know?" he said. "One minute you're getting up from your bust up with the cab, the next thing a goddamned police helicopter drops on the street." He was shaken up, badly, but had still retained the good sense to get himself inside and drag Cal's unconscious body with him.

"How long have I been out?" Cal asked, tenderly feeling the sore swelling on the back of his head. *Nothing broken,* he reassured himself as he tested the movement of his neck, *I don't think so anyway.* Checking himself out from head to toe, Cal decided that he was pretty beaten up but still functional. Patting his pockets to make sure he still had everything, Cal glanced up at the man to prompt an answer.

"I don't know. A couple minutes, tops?" said the man who was watching the inferno in the street through his shop window.

Shit, Cal thought, *I need to get the hell out of here.*

Rising slowly, he found that his feet still worked, just about, and he walked carefully to the front door.

"Whoa, Jesus, you can't go out there! I can't even get through on 911 but you need a doctor or something," said the man holding up both hands.

"I have to get back to the hotel," Cal said, entertaining no further delays. "North on 3rd, left onto 23rd for two blocks and right onto Park?" he said.

The man hesitated, but shrugged. "Yeah, but you need to be careful. It's nuts out there, I mean real pandemonium."

"I'll be careful," Cal said, reaching for the door. He paused, turned his stiff neck to the man who watched his neighborhood with concern out the window. "Thank you," he said.

The man shrugged again. "Forget about it. Welcome to New York, huh?"

REGULAR SUPERHERO

Friday 2:55 p.m. - 23rd Street, NYC

Cal staggered around the corner, glanced up at the four-way signpost to confirm he was on the right street, and shuffled his feet west. He had wandered in a daze through the city, screams and sirens echoing on every street. Everywhere he looked he saw emergency first responders rushing around, and it seemed impossible to Cal that there were even more people in the streets than there were before. If his brain had registered the facts, if he wasn't suffering with back-to-back concussions both sustained inside an hour of each other, then he might have realized that it was because nobody was using the subway.

He didn't know that the subway was shut down. That the entire city limits and beyond were a no-fly zone for any aircraft under threat of being shot down by the US Naval aviators screaming high above in a figure-eight holding pattern. He didn't know that every bridge and tunnel was on lockdown not only because of a suspicious number of simultaneous fires but also by the authorities. Only the Brooklyn Bridge remained undamaged, and the NYPD hadn't got there in time to close it, so people streamed off the island as fast as they could on foot over the bridge and in the south by every available ferry.

Those that remained on the island, those who weren't trying to escape, were shutting up their homes and businesses as an air of fear and foreboding descended over the city.

The NYPD, an almost forty-thousand strong army of law enforcement, expertly trained in anti-terror drills and well equipped, worked tirelessly. Those who weren't actively involved in the cleanup operation or securing the scenes of the bombings, were either patrolling the streets to keep the peace or else preparing for the night. Experience dictated that public disorder, looting and mayhem, would likely take over during the darkness. Every man and woman of the department, unless already committed, was making their way to their station houses to protect their city.

Cal, despite his obviously battered appearance having been blown up, run down, and narrowly avoided having a helicopter land on his head, wandered the streets without anyone giving him a second glance for whole blocks at a time. Now, reaching the end of the second block he had walked on 23rd as he called them aloud to himself, he was approached by someone in jeans and a dark bomber jacket.

"Sir, are you okay? Are you hurt?" the young man said in a voice of clear professional intensity. His left hand was held out toward Cal with the palm outwards and his right hand was worryingly out of sight inside his jacket.

"Sir, can you tell me what happened?" he said again.

Cal faced him, holding up both hands as though his exhaustion had overtaken him and he was surrendering. "I'm just trying to get to my hotel," he told the man who, now that he looked at him closely, seemed more of a boy than a man. Cal guessed he was in his early twenties at best, and guessed from his speech and body language that he was a cop. The young man had dropped a black bag at his feet to allow him effective use of both hands, and Cal guessed that he wasn't expecting to get home for a shower and a change of clothes any time soon.

"Sir," said the man again, "what happened to you?"

Cal sighed, knowing that he wasn't going to be allowed to go until he had satisfied the evident rookie's curiosity. "I was on Wall Street earlier," he told him, "and there was a bomb in the subway. Then I got hit by a cab and then a helicopter crashed next to me. I just need to get to my hotel."

"Sir, you need medical attention and then I need to interview you as a witness." He produced a badge from a pocket with his left hand, bearing the shield logo of the NYPD.

"I don't need medical attention," Cal told him, "I need to go."

"Sir!" the cop said, shuffling one pace backwards quickly as Cal had closed the gap by taking one step forwards. "Keep your hands where they are and stay back!"

"Oh, for fuck sake!" Cal snapped, regretting raising his voice as his head throbbed again. "Look, I'm not a threat, I'm not a terrorist and I need to get to my hotel."

The young police officer was clearly torn between getting to his duty station and dealing with the situation he had caused. "Okay, sir. I'm going to need you to tell me your name and give me the details of your hotel so someone can ask you a few questions."

"Fine," Cal answered, "Owen Calhoun, and I'm staying at the Waldorf."

"*The* Waldorf?" the cop answered, his surprise evident.

"Yes," Cal said, tired and dizzy again now that his momentum had been lost.

"I'm Officer Peters from the One-Three," he told Cal, as though the information would mean anything to him.

"Okay, Officer Peters. Can I go now?" he asked.

Peters hesitated, trying to figure out if keeping hold of this potential witness was his duty or whether he should wait for orders. He weighed up the pros and cons of the decision; if he let the guy go and he disappeared, then he would've walked away from a witness or maybe even a suspect. If he didn't get to the station house four blocks away on 21st Street, then he would never live it down.

He wasn't due on duty until the following Monday, but there was an unwritten rule that when something big happens, you got your ass to the house and rolled out. Eventually deciding that he could spare a couple hours at least before he walked into the precinct to report for extra duty, he stood and relaxed his stance.

"Yeah, but I'm going to see that you get back to your hotel first," he told Cal as he stooped to pick up the heavy bag and loop it over his shoulder. "We're about twenty blocks away. Reckon you can make a couple miles?" he asked Cal, who nodded and limped next to him as fast as was sustainable.

The panic in the streets was sometimes obvious, sometimes less so. All around people were crying and trying to make phone calls, and the steady flow of first responders heading south with lights and sirens blazing had a clear effect on Officer Peters, who seemed to want to leap into action like a superhero and save the world. Other people wandered almost nonchalantly, as though panicking was beneath them.

"You're new, aren't you Officer Peters?" Cal asked him, the question coming out a little less politely than intended.

"I'm in my second year with the NYPD," he replied, clearly taking no offence. "Moved here four years ago." Cal couldn't place his accent but he had guessed he wasn't native.

"My family's from New Hampshire," he said, anticipating the question. "I kind of upset the family tradition by wanting to be a cop," he admitted.

"What's the family business then?" Cal asked, not out of anything other than to pass the time as they skirted Grand Central Station and the crowds trying to get on trains which weren't running.

"Wines and beers," Peters said. "My father's company owns a large distribution network and expected me and my brothers to take over the empire," he told Cal with a smile. Something told the Englishman that the kid enjoyed upsetting the apple cart. "Told my dad I wanted to be a cop, and he went nuts. Then I told him I wanted to be a New York cop and he popped his cork. And it's Jake."

"Cal," Cal replied. "So, he kicked you out and you went and did it anyway?"

"Kinda," Jake replied, "my mom set me up with enough money to get a place here and didn't tell my dad. She understands why I wanted to do this."

"Why did you?" Cal asked, now interested in the answer as to why this young, rich kid wanted to be on the frontline.

Jake sighed before answering. "I was in the first grade when 9-11 happened. I remember watching it on TV and seeing what the first responders did to save people. Ever since then I wanted to be like them: someone who runs *toward* the danger instead of away from it."

He stopped talking, making Cal suspect that the word 'hero' was on the tip of his tongue but he didn't want to say it for fear of embarrassment.

"Well I think that's noble," Cal said, feeling embarrassed himself at having spoken his thoughts.

"Thanks," Jake said, smiling at him, just as a scream pierced the afternoon air and sliced through the cacophony of a city in panic. Jake dropped his bag and drew his compact Glock 26 from the holster under his left arm; every man and woman of his squad carried a weapon off duty, wherever they were in the state, the only exception being when they were partying. Even then, their designated drivers usually had their off-duty carries with them.

"Stay here," he hissed over his shoulder as he moved to the corner and peeked around it. Whipping his head back into cover he took three deep breaths and spun back again, disappearing into the side street. Cal moved to the corner where Jake had been and looked around. He saw the young cop moving low and using the cover of a dumpster to mask his approach, but in the background, he saw a woman struggling with a man far taller than she was, both fighting over her purse.

"Gimme the bag, bitch!" Cal heard, just as Jake stood up from cover and shouted, "NYPD, FREEZE!"

The would-be robber didn't freeze. He fled without hesitation, deciding that the night would probably have far better spoils than just this one purse. He had no way of knowing that Jake was off-duty and had no backup; he just ran. Cal limped out into sight having picked up Jake's bag and followed as he saw the young cop approach the woman. She was sobbing on the ground as she tried to put the spilled contents of her purse back in.

"Ma'am, are you alright? Are you hurt?" Jake said, holding his badge out to show her but still scanning the street ahead with his gun raised. The woman tried to wipe her tears away but they were replaced as quickly as they were gone. She was sobbing and terrified, but tried to smile and nod her head to say she was okay.

By the time Cal had caught up with them he saw her nod turn into a shake of her head and the tears flowed again.

"We need to get you inside somewhere," Cal said to her, bending down and offering her a hand.

Jake holstered the stubby, compact sidearm behind inside his jacket again and picked up the bag. "Ma'am, I need to call this in only I can't get through when I try." He turned to Cal. "We're only a couple blocks from your hotel, we should get there, and I'll try to get a unit to us." For the first time Cal saw real concern on Jake's face, like his bravery and bravado was a front and, just like everyone else, he was scared. Cal also noticed that he had failed to mention not being able to contact his precinct by phone. Coupled with the man who dragged him away from the helicopter wreckage saying that the 911 phone system was down, Cal began to suspect that the bombs may just be the start.

"Come on," Jake said to them both before turning to the woman who was attempting to straighten her disheveled appearance. "Ma'am, I'm Officer Jake Peters and this is Mr. Owen Calhoun from England," he told her, introducing Cal so formally that he actually felt a little ashamed of his shabby and battered appearance.

"We're going to get you to the Waldorf hotel where I can call for a bus to check you both out." She nodded weakly and walked with them. Jake turned to Cal and thanked him for his help.

"I didn't do anything!" Cal told him, thinking that if Jake hadn't been there then he wouldn't have been able to offer much in the way of protection.

"Maybe not," Jake told him, "but you came with me and saved my gear. I appreciate that."

Cal said nothing in response, embarrassed at being told he had done a good thing. The three walked slowly the remainder of the way to the Waldorf, mainly due to the crying woman with her shaking legs. Arriving at the entrance they found it locked. Jake banged on the glass, showing his badge to the nervous-looking security guard inside.

Another man, taller and wearing a crisply cut gray suit, strode over, and shot the bolts back.

"Cal?" he said. "What the hell happened to you?"

The three of them piled inside and the doors were locked again.

"Got blown up," he said glibly, "then I got knocked down by a cab, then a helicopter crashed next to me." Somehow, reducing the last few hours of his life to these three events summed it up perfectly, and Sebastian's usually unfazed exterior showed shock.

"Sir," said Jake, taking charge of the conversation, "Officer Peters from the One-Three. We rescued this civilian nearby and I believe she needs medical attention."

"Of course," Sebastian answered. "Please, this way." He gestured them further inside the lobby where he snapped his fingers at a member of his staff. She disappeared and returned quickly bearing a first aid kit as Cal sat the woman down on a comfortable chair.

"Sir, may I have a word with you in private?" Jake said softly to Sebastian, who wordlessly led the way back to the main desk. Cal didn't seem to have been invited to join in the conversation, but similarly he wasn't asked to stay out of it, so he followed the two men.

"I'll be straight with you, I can't contact my station house by telephone. I need to get a unit here to take the statement of Mr.

Calhoun who witnessed the attacks and to deal with the attempted robbery of the lady back there." Sebastian took all this in and nodded.

"Perhaps, Officer Peters, you'd care to try again from here?" he said, gesturing to the telephone on the desk.

"Yes, sir," he answered, picking up the handset only to put it down again. "Line's dead," he told them. Pausing and hesitating, Jake looked them both in the eye. "I'm going back on foot, I'll get back here as soon as I can," he told them. "Sir, what's your security situation here?" he asked Sebastian.

"I have four guards in the building and we are currently on lockdown. I know our guests so I'll admit them if they return but other than that we will be keeping everyone inside the building." Jake nodded. He turned to Cal. "I'll be back as soon as I can to get your statement about today's events," he said formally, robotically, before he turned to the door.

"Jake," Cal said, making the young cop turn back to face him, "be careful."

"Don't you worry about me, sir," he said with a smile which he hoped made him seem confident.

Picking up his bag, he slung it on his back using the side straps like a backpack and nodded to the guard. The bolts shot back and Jake jogged out into the failing sunlight, turned left, and went to run the fifteen blocks to his station house. Cal's memory kicked him square in the chest then, and he turned back to Sebastian, putting a hand on his shoulder.

"My, er, guest who stayed last night," he said awkwardly. "Did she make it back?"

"Cal," Sebastian replied seriously, "I haven't let her back in since we locked the building down. We've turned away a few people who wanted to get inside but I swear to you I haven't seen her."

Cal limped toward the elevators as quickly as he could, cursing the slow speed as he went up. He pushed out of the sliding doors before they were fully open, stomped to his door, and let himself in with the key card.

Inside, the bed had been made but Louise wasn't there. His heart dropped in his chest, making him feel cold and weak. The thought of her still out there, with the sun sinking and people already starting to commit crime at higher rates than normal, crushed him. He sank to the floor, too exhausted to cry, and his eyes rested on something by the bed. It wasn't his, and it wasn't there when he left. It was a large, battered backpack.

The bathroom door opened and she walked out, dropping the towel she was using to dry her hair the second she saw him.

"Oh my god, Cal, what the hell y'all been doing to yourself?" she said desperately, dropping to her knees and taking his face in her hands.

"Got blown up," Cal said, "then I got knocked down by a cab, and then a helicopter crashed on me." His rehearsed version of simplified events rolled off his tongue easily, like he knew he'd be retelling that story many times over in his life.

Louise wrapped him up in a tight hug, feeling the spasmodic convulsions of a grown man crying into her shoulder.

EXPECT NOTHING

Friday 5:20 p.m. - Free America Movement Headquarters

"Colonel Butler, sir?" said an aide, sporting acne-scarred cheeks and a confused but expectant look on his face.

"What is it, son?" Butler said, the evident success of the New York phase making him feel more inclined to talk.

"Sir," stammered the boy, pointing at one of the screens, "did we do that?"

Butler's eyes followed the outstretched digit, resting on one of the silent televisions which now showed mostly darkness. Fumbling for the remotes he tried to turn the sound on, growling at Suzanne who tried to step forward and take it from his hand to make it work. He finally found the sound controls and cranked it up.

"... *can see here, whole city blocks are in darkness as the power is shutting down. Still no word on who was responsible for the attacks, but so far we know that six*"—she put a finger to hear earpiece and paused momentarily as she glanced down—"*no, seven explosions have occurred in the city, five of which have been confirmed as having been at subway entrances—*"

The reporter stumbled as three or four people barged through their street-side film setup, jostling the cameraman who managed to regain himself and point the lens back at the anchor.

"You good? We still on?" she asked the man behind the camera, evidently getting the correct answer as she switched her gaze back down the lens and resumed her report.

"As I said, five confirmed explosions happened in subway tunnels and some mixed reports have come in saying that the stock exchange itself was the target. In fact, all attacks have been in and around the financial district of the city. Nobody has taken responsibility for the truck fires which blocked the bridges and tunnels, and NYPD press officers have not yet made any arrests in connection with the events earlier today. We have had confirmation that the NYPD's air support has come under attacks and is unable to fly, with two helicopters having crashed in the city with the tragic loss of all lives onboard ..."

The news anchor trailed off as the lights of every shop in the street failed, flickering into darkness. Despite the sun not having set, the sudden absence of artificial lighting inside the city's man-made valleys between the high buildings made everything so much more sinister. The background noise of car horns tripled in intensity as every traffic light in the city died.

The reporter regained herself, flicking her hair out of her eyes and fixing her best 'brave woman on the ground in a crisis' face toward the camera lens. *"As far as we know, no organization or person has yet to take credit for the attacks, and—"*

She never got to finish her sentence.

Behind her, even before the shockwave and the flying debris and shattered glass had a chance to fly across the road to her, the blossoming fire of an explosion grew from inside the plate glass of a department store. Before the feed was cut, the final recorded frame was frozen on the screen, still bearing the banner 'LIVE' as the reporter's hair had caught fire and the flesh was burned from her cheek. That gruesome, grotesque, and horrifying freeze-frame was suspended for a few seconds, showing the world an uncomfortably close-up view of a woman being blown to pieces. The screen went black.

Butler carefully put down the TV remote he had been clutching, lining it up at perfect angles with the others, and stood tall.

"To answer your first question, son: No. The power outages aren't us," he said, straightening the uniformed shirt he wore.

"And to answer the second question you haven't yet asked: No. That bomb wasn't us either. We had five backpack devices for the subways, one small IED, and one RPG for the diversion. So no, son, we did not knock out the power and we did not blow up that reporter." He walked away, head high but mind on fire.

Sitting at his desk to try and find some space for his brain to react to what he had just witnessed, he clenched the fingers of his left hand into a fist to stop it shaking.

"Unexpected bonus?" Suzanne's voice asked carefully, interrupting his moment of internal concern.

"What?" Butler asked her, almost angry that she would feel the loss of an innocent life was anything but a tragic necessity in the fight for their freedom.

"I mean the power outages," she said, her face showing an equal distain that he might think she enjoyed watching the reporter get killed. "Won't a blackout accelerate the timeline? Create chaos in the city quicker?"

"Yes," Butler replied, leaning back and backing down, "it certainly will do that."

"So, this is a good thing?" Suzanne offered carefully, trying to massage Butler's ego into accepting her way of thinking. "Better than expected?"

"Suzanne," Butler said seriously, "I expect nothing— *nothing*—but that my men do the things asked of them. If the plan fails and men have done their duty, then the fault lies with command." With that, Butler had evidently ended the conversation.

Suzanne walked away, angry at pompous military men with their fatalistic views on actionable problems. Maybe they didn't make all the mess in the city right now, but the plan was to shut down the money, close off the island as much as possible and let it tear itself apart for a night. After that the president and his senior staff, all of whom were under the strict protection of

Major Taylor's unit in Washington, would issue instruction for the military to reestablish order.

After seeing how badly the Movement could damage the infrastructure, of how connected and powerful they were, the new era could begin.

Butler could almost see it now, as he was brought in as the national security advisor to the president. He would have key members of the Movement everywhere, and they would puppet the existing administration through fear of their ability to bring instability. It would be a perfect, near silent *coup d'état*.

Taylor's men had already succeeded in securing POTUS, and the whole area was locked down after the White House reported that a terror attack on the president had been foiled by National Guardsmen. Those same guardsmen had the senior politicians secured underground and would be heralded as heroes who acted on instinct and stormed the White House to save the day.

The truth was what the newspapers reported after the shit had hit the fan, just as history had always been written by the victors.

Saturday 5:20 a.m. Local Time, Beijing

The stony-faced woman in the dark suit barely blinked as her eyes scanned the wall of screens. Occasionally she would shout a number, and the corresponding television would play the sound through disassociated speakers until she had heard enough. She waved a hand for the sound to be turned off again and took her eyes away for a second to make sure she connected the tip of the cigarette to the intense flame jetting out of the windproof lighter.

Eyes flicking back up, she pocketed the lighter and rested an elbow on her hip as she smoked, digging the fingernails of her right hand into the pad of her thumb one by one. The small pain helped to focus her, helped her to stay alert and connected. It was a thing she did when she was tired, when she needed to concentrate, and at times she had even drawn blood.

A man stopped as he walked past her, turned to follow his nose in the darkened room and opened his mouth to protest about her smoking inside the control room. Before any words left his mouth, his brain saved him from pain and humiliation and he closed it in silence. In a building where not wearing identification could get you searched at gunpoint and dragged off site, the fact that she wore nothing indicating she had a right to be there worried him deeply. Only people from certain walks of life could get away with being in this building and so obviously flaunt their anonymity. He decided that if this ghost wanted to smoke in the control room, then it wasn't for him to offer an opinion otherwise.

Walking away as the woman took another long drag and smiled at the back of his retreating head, she saw him kick the chair of an analyst who was leaning back to stretch, and heard him bark orders for the analyst to keep working and not to relax.

Kick the cat? the woman thought, *is that what the English say?*

"There! Thirty-six," she said, her voice deeper and more powerful than her small stature would indicate.

"Take it back and show me," she snapped, dropping her half-smoked cigarette into the glass of water in her other hand, and reaching out to swap the glass for a large tablet the analyst held. The swap didn't materialize immediately, so her fingers snapped twice to indicate that everyone around her was failing.

The pad appeared, and she tapped the screen to play footage of an up-close version of what she had just seen at a distance, only this time with sound. Her finger swiped across the bottom of the screen, replaying the explosion frame by frame with each tap of a delicate digit, and a smile crept across her face. Almost throwing the pad back, she stalked back to the corner she had been stood in and spoke over her shoulder to the shadows behind.

"Our assets are in play," she said. "Power grid is failing and secondary explosions have begun. By tomorrow the American puppets will have lost any credibility they could have gained and there will be chaos." She reached back into the pocket of her suit jacket, retrieving another cigarette and the miniature flamethrower she used to light it. A snap of fingers from the recess behind her echoed, making her hand back the one she had just lit and incinerate the tip of another for herself.

"Activate the rest. All of them," said a voice even more menacing than her own. "Let them tear themselves apart for now and then we will turn the vise tighter."

She half-cocked her head toward the source of the orders, nodded slightly in a bow of acknowledgment, and walked away.

Friday 6:40 p.m. – New York City

The man flipped up the rubberized antenna of his satellite phone and answered the call with a single word.

He listened, repeating his acknowledgment two more times, before ending the call and stowing the phone in his backpack. Six other men and three women were in the room in Midtown with him, and all eyes were on him.

"We go soon," he said, "when it is darker." He walked through the room and made eye contact with his whole team as he went.

"Any target is legitimate," he told them. "NYPD, National Guard, banks, shops, local thugs. We tear this city down. Work your sectors in pairs, stay out of sight, and be back here before sunrise."

He knew his team wouldn't be the only one active that night, and he reiterated their area of operations, their limits of exploitation, nervous that they would end up in a firefight with another team of insurgents intent on their own goals of destabilization and carnage.

The eight other people in the room all stood and sketched a bow at the man in charge, before pairing off and preparing to head out to the areas allocated to them. They would spend the night sniping at police patrols, throwing grenades into shop windows and setting fires. None of them doubted that many residents of the city would take very little encouragement to riot, but they had been activated to accelerate the process.

It had been a simple thing to overload the power relays remotely and shut down the supply to the city. Now nothing that didn't have its own generator would be dark, and anything that did would attract a load of attention it probably didn't want.

Chung Fei, thirty-one years old, unmarried, and a dedicated servant to his beloved country, checked the top pocket of his backpack as his team prepared themselves similarly. He smiled at the sight of the fifteen incendiary grenades within easy reach. Having spent months working in the city being treated like dirt, he had more than a few places in mind he wanted to pay a visit to that night.

HOLDING PATTERN

Friday 6:58 p.m. - Ninety-Eight Hundred Feet Over NYC

"Phantom this is Banjo, here to relieve you, over," came the southern drawl over the F-35 pilot's headset. He still had almost forty-five minutes playtime on station before he and his wing-man would be bingo-fuel and in any other setting he would want to stay up in the sky hunting.

Today was different.

"Banjo, Phantom," he said with none of the bravado of his fellow fighter jock. "Skies are all yours, we are RTB. Stay Safe and stay high. Phantom out."

"Wilco, Phantom. Go get a cold one for me," replied the fresh pilot as he banked hard left in his holding pattern to get a satellite view of Manhattan. Only he couldn't see the island. He could barely see anything below without switching to use the fighter's high-tech array of sensors, but even at this height he expected to be able to see the outline of the island.

Levelling out and keeping his plane in the wide figure-eight that the previous two pilots had worked their duration, Christopher 'Banjo' Redden mentally prepared himself for the next five hours of dull inactivity as he screamed around the skies above New York at close to three hundred miles per hour, waiting for his relief to come at midnight.

Friday 7:20 p.m. – 13th Precinct Station House

"Sarge, I'm telling you, this guy saw it happen," Jake Peters told his overworked supervisor, as though repeating himself would make any difference.

"Look kid," the sergeant said, turning and bumping his considerable gut into Jake's lean frame. "We got car wrecks, the city's in gridlock, we've lost guys in the explosions and in the chopper crashes, and you want me to prioritize some British guy who got himself too close to something that went boom?"

"There's the robbery victim too," Jake said weakly. "Come on, Sarge. It was felony assault right in front of me. I drew my off-duty weapon. I gotta write this up!"

Jake Peters was a pain in the sergeant's ass on most days, but today he just couldn't handle him arguing to fight the good fight just like every other day he'd known the kid.

"Fine. Go get your complaint," he told him. Jake smiled and went to turn away before he was stopped. "Tomorrow," the sergeant said, "because right now I need you up on 23rd stopping traffic coming up the one-way streets, okay?"

Jake never got a chance to answer. For an overweight man, the sergeant really knew how to move when he wanted to.

His deployment was unprecedented as he wasn't usually called to guard street entrances for minor traffic violations, but he guessed that the real reason for it was to try and get a cop on every street corner and not for any traffic-related reason as that responsibility had been farmed outside of the NYPD years before. What was unprecedented, for him at least, was going anywhere on duty alone, but he guessed that needs must.

He sighed as he turned away, knowing that he would be walking the two blocks back to 23rd where he had first met Cal stumbling toward him bleeding. He wished he could take something heavier than the Glock, if only to reassure himself. He doubted the general population would feel similarly reassured.

It would definitely reassure me, he thought, convincing himself that it was a childish want to take one of the shotguns stored at the station house, even though he got a foreboding feeling that he may require more firepower before the night was out. Jake stood rooted to the spot, trying to find a way to get through to his supervisor and be permitted to return to the Waldorf, but he sighed and did as he was told. The lights in the station house flickered, going dark briefly before they weakly returned to life.

He was scared, and the fear was almost as intense as his need to help people, to be the hero, only now that his chance came he felt the fear pulling him away more than he hoped it would. Against all regulations, and more out of fear than anything else, Jake took the harness to hold his off-duty weapon and put it on under his uniform jacket. He carried his service weapon, a Glock 19, which was effectively the same gun just not shrunk down, and the three full magazines for it. Wishing he could still carry something heavier, he made for the door and walked north toward his post.

It took him three times the normal walking distance to make the two blocks. Every second person stopped him to ask what was going on, if he had seen someone who they were looking for, if he could help them.

After barely being able to move for the mob around him wanting answers in the growing dark, he raised his voice and held up both hands to get their attention.

"People, please return to your homes and lock your doors. The NYPD is doing everything we can to find out what's going on. Please, go home."

He tried to walk on, to push through the crowds of scared people—the people he had sworn to protect—but he heard more questions shouted at him.

Why don't the phones work? When is the power going to be restored? Who did this to us?

Jake had no answers to anything, he only repeated his advice for them to return to their homes and lock the doors until this had passed. He hoped that sounding confident would make the people believe him, like he was repeating official advice from the department, and they wouldn't think that he was just as scared and clueless as they were.

He turned up the dial on his radio to hear the traffic in his earpiece but heard nothing. That was unheard of for any time of any day, let alone late on a Friday when the city was in panic. He pulled the radio from its pouch on his belt and checked he was on the right channel. He was, but it was dead. He tried to call up for a commo-check but there was no answer. Trying to convince himself that it was just a black spot, one which hadn't been there on any day of the last year and a half he'd worked this precinct, he pulled his cell from his pocket. Also dead. Nothing which required a signal still worked, but Jake pushed it all aside and told himself that he would get to his post and do his job until he was needed elsewhere.

That kind of delusional thinking got him through almost two hours of yelling, pointing, and being shouted at on 23rd Street. He yelled at drivers to leave their cars after the first six people tried to drive the wrong way down streets to get through the traffic. Desperation did funny things to normally law-abiding citizens, and the thought of abandoning the car they had worked hard to afford was unimaginable to most people, and Jake had argued repeatedly until he realized that the cars which had piled down the wrong way only added to the gridlock on the avenues heading south and north.

People left their cars and walked, carrying their belongings, their children, even their pets.

"Hey!" a male voice snapped from behind him petulantly. Jake turned to see a man in a suit, carrying a briefcase as he stepped out from the back of a stranded town car.

"Hey!" he said again, testing Jake's patience.

"Can I help you, sir?" Jake said, professional but with a hint of steel in his voice.

"You could do your damned job and get these cars outta my way," the man said, earning himself a place at the absolute head of Jake's shit list. Before he could answer, the man compounded his problem.

"Are the ferries to Jersey still running?" he snapped, shooting a cuff and checking his watch before looking back to Jake with wide eyes as though he was absolutely certain the officer was an idiot. He began to repeat his question pronouncing each word slowly.

"I don't know, sir," Jake said with a formality which was intended to shame the obnoxious businessman into changing his attitude.

"Well, get on your little radio and find out from someone who does know then," he ordered Jake, as though his undisclosed status gave him the right to commandeer a New York City police officer for his own errands.

"Can't do that," Jake answered, dropping the 'sir' as he decided the man didn't deserve even a sarcastic amount of manners.

"What do you mean, you can't do that?" said the man, his face cracking into anger.

"I mean, *sir*," Jake said, leaning forward toward him and re-inserting the sarcasm, "that police radios are down. So are the phones. And the city is in gridlock." He let that hang, seeing the anger on his opponent's face sag into something nearing abject fear. "So, I'd suggest that if you want to find out if the Jersey ferry is running, then take a walk and find out for yourself." He relaxed, stood more upright and continued. "Alternatively, you could get your ass back to whatever building you came from and stay indoors until this mess is cleaned up."

The man said nothing. His mouth opened and closed twice, wordlessly, then he straightened himself and went to walk back to the rear of the town car to wait in conditions more befitting his status.

He never made it.

A burst of gunfire erupted from a first-floor window, indiscriminate in aim and intended only to make the street below ignite into instant panic. A single round punctured the throat of the businessman, sending a flood of hot sticky blood down the collar of his hundred-dollar shirt, over the knot of his sixty-dollar tie, making his body drop back to the sidewalk as he choked out on his own blood.

His last memory on earth was someone pausing long enough to relieve him of his twelve-thousand-dollar watch before he took his last bubbling breath, and died.

A fire broke out, unnaturally quickly, in the back seat of the car he had been aiming to spend the remainder of the crisis in, set off by a muted explosion. Jake didn't see it, but he heard it as he tried desperately to get innocent people off the street and into cover. He thought he'd already seen some crazy shit today, but his nightmare was only just beginning to unfold.

ACTIVE SHOOTER

Friday 9:30 p.m. - Park Avenue

Cal and the rest of the guests of the Waldorf were called to a meeting in the large restaurant. Sebastian told all the assembled guests what he knew, reiterated that they had onsite security, and told them that the plan was to hold tight until everything was back to normal.

Questions fired at him, but Cal didn't hear them. He turned to Louise, who regarded him quizzically.

"Why the hell aren't y'all more concerned about this situation, Cal?" she asked him seriously, using her individual way of employing far more words than were necessary for the sentence she spoke. His almost satisfied smile annoyed her when he answered.

"After everything I've survived today, I'm just happy you're safe and we're holed up somewhere nice," he told her. She shot him a tense look and turned away.

"Excuse me? Mr. Sebastian, sir?" she called out as she held her hand aloft. Sebastian heard the sweet, honey-like voice cut through the din of questions, and nodded to her to continue.

"Mind if I ask what the authorities say about all this?" she asked, provoking a rolling mumble of agreement amongst the other guests.

Sebastian held his hands up for quiet so he could answer the question. He had no intention of bullshitting them.

"There is no word from the authorities as yet," he told them, raising his hands higher to hush the response, "and you all know the cell phone and land lines are out of service. So is the city power grid but we have backup power to last another couple of days." His next line was cut off, as the sound of smashing glass echoed from the reception area. Cal and Louise were sat toward the back of the group closest to reception, and Cal thought that he heard the butcher's sound of meat being tenderized, followed by the sound of something heavy hitting the deck.

Before anyone could react, three armed men rounded the ornate archway into the restaurant and brandished their weapons.

"Okay bitches, none of you assholes move," declared the evident leader, a head shorter than his thugs and with an accent that told Cal he was trying hard to be American by very recent way of Eastern Europe. He remembered being told that the Polish gangs were as prevalent as the famous mobsters and mafia groups which were the stuff of film legends. Real organized crime was less Hollywood, and far more frightening in real life.

"We are going to be wanting your jewels and your cash," he said, taking the lit cigarette from his mouth, and dropping it onto the expensive carpet, "and don't any of you motherfuckers try anything … *heroic*." He smiled, clearly impressed with himself for his mastery of the English language.

Cal and Louise looked to each other. Between them they probably had less than fifty dollars and no jewels to speak of. Certainly not the kind of Omega, Breitling and Cartier watches the other guests were reluctantly slipping from their shaking wrists and trying to hide, along with the diamonds hanging from the ears of the women Cal, and he was certain the gang, could see. He had been told, interestingly by someone he worked with who had never visited New York or even the States, that he should always keep his 'robbery money' to hand. He hadn't bothered, on the basis that he thought the guy was full of shit, but now he saw the sense in having something tangible to hand to ward off anything like this.

He stole a glance at the leather-jacketed, gold-chain-wearing goons who were starting to work the room. The only guns he saw were sawed-off shotguns which he knew were devastatingly brutal up close but merely frightening—okay, *very* frightening—at any kind of distance. Tucked in the waistband of the smaller man who had given the orders was the black plastic and chrome butt of a semi-auto pistol which Cal didn't recognize. Not that he needed to; a gun was a gun, and he didn't have one.

~

Jake ducked his head back out of cover to snatch a glance at the building where the gunfire came from. He saw the ground floor communal door open, and a dark figure burst from it before turning left and running.

"Gun!" he said to himself instinctively, as though he were working with backup who needed that prevalent information. A second shape popped up from between the cars having thrown an incendiary grenade into the open window of a long, black car, and followed the other.

"NYPD!" Jake screamed as he broke cover, Glock raised and held out in front of him in two hands.

The response was not what he was expecting, even though he wasn't sure they would just surrender to him. As one, both shapes turned and dropped low, popping up in a different place and unleashing hell. He didn't so much hear the gunfire as feel the stinging air pulse around him as the bullets cracked past.

Suppressed weapons, he thought to himself, *subsonic rounds*.

This intelligence update didn't help him, as he was facing two well-armed suspects both firing automatic weapons when all he had was three mags for his service weapons and two for the smaller piece tucked in the rig under his left armpit. He dropped and rolled, taking cover behind the engine block of an abandoned cab before rising to his knee and looking for a target. They were gone, and all around him the street erupted in more chaos as the fire grew behind him and people's screams pierced the night. He thought that someone behind him may have been hit because the screams from that direction swelled in pitch and intensity, but his priority was the shooters.

A massive part of his training had been dedicated to this. An active shooter scenario was something that was practiced and trained to law enforcement across most of the world. He remembered, vividly, being made to sit through the footage from Mumbai where a guy with an AK and a thousand rounds of 7.62 had run riot like a one-man army until he was put down. The damage a single man or woman could do with an automatic weapon was incredible, even worse in places like the UK where most cops relied on pepper spray and a stern talking to rather than firearms. Now he was faced with an active shooter situation, without backup, and he was outgunned by not one but both shooters.

He had sworn an oath, and he couldn't allow himself to hide or run away.

The problem with the war on terror in any setting, be that war or in a scenario like Jake found himself, was that of rules. Jake had to justify every pull of his trigger, and he was identifiable by his uniform. His enemy, on the other hand, wore no uniform and abided by no rules that anyone knew of. They could kill, could murder, with impunity whereas he might walk straight by an enemy combatant and not even realize. When facing those limitations and those kinds of odds, the Western world was already losing the fight.

Except now he had a clear view of his quarry as they sprinted north. He followed, unthinkingly, only this time he didn't announce his presence and wait to be fired on first to justify his actions. As far as he was concerned, he had already given them fair warning of who he was, and anyone in NYC who didn't fully comprehend that firing an automatic weapon at an officer of the NYPD would result in lethal force being used against them was just plain tired of living. Or prepared for martyrdom, he thought more worryingly.

He knew that any further verbal warnings, or pointless shouts for them to freeze, would only result in them turning and laying down more fire at him, and that would mean endangering the lives of the people running to get off the street. Keeping low, he saw the lead shadow turn and take a knee, scanning the street in his direction over a rifle barrel. Jake dropped flat, skidding on the sidewalk and losing his hat. Instinctively he reached for the radio on his shoulder, clicking the button but saying nothing. It made no noise and he remembered it was dead.

He was on his own.

~

Cal put his handful of cash in the bag held by the thug who appeared to have been born without a visible neck. His hackles rose as the thug's eyebrows under his receding hairline raised when he took a closer look at Louise beside him. Cal stiffened, but Louise placed a hand on his leg and smiled as she dropped in her handful of small notes and tried to placate the brutal man. He shot one last look of warning to Cal and moved on for greater spoils.

"Don't even think about it," Louise whispered to him. "Y'all ain't big enough to take on these assholes."

Cal didn't care at that moment. He was offended, deeply, right to the core of his very soul, by these goons. Taking his money was one thing, but after what he had survived today already he was sure as hell not going to get killed by some petty thieves, especially not ones who were looking at Louise like they did.

"Gentlemen, please," Cal heard from the front of the room, unmistakably Sebastian's cultured tones. "I implore you not to hurt any of our guests, just take what you want and leave."

Cal groaned inside. As sure as he was that Sebastian had to make the attempt, he knew that the thugs would be highly unlikely to respond positively to being told to—no matter how politely it was phrased—get the fuck out. The lead thug stopped, turned toward the source of the voice, and asked him to repeat himself. Sebastian stood, straightened his jacket, and calmly asked the thugs to go about their intended business and then leave, peacefully.

The thug smiled. "You hear that boys?" he said to his goons, laughing. "The *gentleman* here wishes us to leave peacefully," he sneered, producing the oversized handgun from his waistband and waving it around the room as he spoke. He began to walk toward Sebastian slowly, waving the gun around recklessly in tune with his words as though he were directing some grotesque orchestra. "Well I regret to inform the gentleman that our business will not be concluded for some time," he said, stepping close to Sebastian and craning his neck to look the suave man in the eye. Finding the height difference not to his liking he turned away in a feint, but spun and brought the barrel of his heavy pistol round to crack it across the smug man's face.

Watch this, bitches, he thought to himself triumphantly, baring his teeth with a grunt as he put all his effort into the cheap shot.

His momentum pulled him straight through where the contact should have been, and he wasn't rewarded with the sickening crunch he was anticipating. Instead he spun off balance, half stumbling to the floor tangled in his own feet.

And that was when the strike hit him. It wasn't a punch as such, wasn't a fist hitting him as he had experienced so many times in his life, but was more like being stabbed. Incidentally, that was also something he had experienced more than once in his life, but neither occasion had prepared him for this. A single protruding knuckle impacted just to the left of his windpipe, having the instant effect of removing the last shred of control he had over his feet. Worse still, before he could fulfill the intentions of gravity and hit the plush carpeted ground, a second jab impacted his right eye and blinded him. He finally finished his uncontrolled descent and hit the carpet so hard he bounced up a little. As he spun, in between the two sniper-accurate jabs that rendered him useless, Sebastian had snatched the gun from his hand and raised it to the surprised thugs, switching the aim from one to the other.

Confusion reigned over them, their panic evident in the glances they threw at one another. "Don't!" Sebastian warned them. "Guns on the floor and get out," he told them, waiting a few seconds before racking back the topslide of the weapon. A spinning brass round ejected from the port, showing that the thug already had a bullet chambered, but Sebastian wanted to make sure. He had learned long ago that the psychological effect of the action went a long way to invoke fear, like the unmistakable racking of a pump action shotgun. They both put down their guns and held up their hands.

"And take this"—he paused and shot a sharp kick into the ribs of the moaning, insensible gangster at his feet— "*gentleman* with you," he finished, earning a small giggle from the few guests not paralyzed by fear.

Slowly, cautiously, the goons crept forward and dragged their diminutive boss with them. Sebastian followed them all the way to the shattered window they had used to admit themselves, shooting a glance at his security guard who has down and bleeding from the head. He watched as they retreated into the darkness before giving instructions to block the shattered window with furniture, for his remaining intact security guards to utilize the sawed-off shotguns they had now inherited, and for the injured man to be given medical attention, all before he furrowed his brow and thought hard about their next move. Cal found him there, flanked by Louise, still deep in thought.

"Sebastian," Cal said, almost waking him up from his trance.

"Cal. Yes. Sorry?" he said, regaining his composure.

"Um, you okay?" Cal asked him. "That was some Bruce Lee shit back there, mate …"

"Those self-defense classes paid off I suppose," he responded glibly with a smile which neither of them believed. "If you'll excuse me?" he said before walking away, leaving the two with more questions than answers. They heard orders being given, polite orders but orders all the same, for people to head upstairs away from the ground floor.

~

Jake had dogged the pair of shooters nearly ten blocks like a relentless bloodhound, hoping for a chance to get a shot off or to miraculously bump into some backup. Without communications, he felt totally exposed and more vulnerable than he had ever been in his life. Still, he couldn't let these two go, he couldn't break off his pursuit, but neither could he see a way that this could end well.

Here am I, he recited from the book of Isaiah privately as though the words could steel his resolve and shroud him in righteous armor, *send me.*

Shouts up ahead made him pop his head over the hood of the car he was using as cover, and the responding burst of automatic fire didn't take long to zero in on his position. The noises, the pattern of their cat and mouse engagement had changed somehow, but Jake had yet to figure it out. He heard shouts again, and more muted gunfire from the suppressed weapons he would have nightmares about for the rest of his life, but none of the shots fired came in his direction this time; they were engaged to their front.

Creeping low to the rear of a car, he sprinted across to the other side of the street without looking first so as not to give away his new position. He didn't stop until he threw himself hard into the opposite sidewalk and tucked into cover. He hadn't been seen, and hopefully the shooter who had taken a pop at him would not be expecting him on this side. Staying low, he moved toward the shouts and gunfire until he could hear the grunts and breathing of his suspects. Tucked in low with his back up against the front wheel of a car, Jake took three long and slow breaths to steady himself.

Peeking out, he saw the back of one of the shooters as he took cover behind a car up ahead, easily within accurate range of his Glock. He closed his eyes momentarily and stood.

He leveled his weapon, aiming for center mass, but couldn't pull the trigger. Despite the crazy events, he couldn't just execute a man in cold blood.

"NYPD, put your weapons on the ground, NOW!" he called out, sounding less authoritative than he intended. The shooter did not comply. Simultaneously spinning and dropping to the ground, a burst of gunfire erupted over Jake's head and missed him by a hand's breadth. His own answering shots, two solid hits to the chest, dropped the shooter.

He moved forward, eyes scanning ahead in fear of the second gunman. Taking a knee beside his suspect, he switched the Glock to a one-handed grip and put two fingers to the throat of the man. He felt warm skin, smooth where it should be stubbled, and glanced down. He saw two eyes wide open, not in death but alert. His own shock had no time to register this, even though body armor was something that he should've anticipated, and a reflected flash sparkled in front of his eye as a knife came toward him.

He had no time to disengage and use his sidearm. Had no time to issue a warning or use any of the disarming techniques he had been taught. Instead he acted instinctively, smashing the butt of his gun down on the face beside his knee. The crunch of bone sickened him, as did the sticky, metallic smell of the hot liquid on his hand, but the knife dropped with a clang to the street.

A shout ahead, too close for comfort, made his eyes snap up and into the fat, bulbous barrel of a stubby rifle aimed at him. Jake closed his eyes, and waited for oblivion.

AS USELESS AS THE 'G' IN LASAGNE

Major Taylor and his team had secured the White House along with all the senior members of staff. The president was livid, threatening each and every man with the death penalty for treason. Taylor was worried that he would start to have a negative effect on the moral of his troops, so he isolated him under the guard of two of his most trusted men.

Taylor acted confidently, but he did not feel at all confident. The longer their secret siege went on, the higher the risks of failure were. By now, events in New York were on schedule, and already the impact on the world financial market was huge. They were crippling their own country, albeit temporarily, but they did what they did for the greater good and the long-term prosperity of their beloved United States of America.

"Major, this is Johnson. Over," came the squelch from his earpiece on their closed squad-net radio.

"Go," came the terse response.

"Sir, the president would like to speak with you at your earliest convenience," Johnson, an implacable if somewhat unthinking sergeant under his command, told him. It was one of the reasons he chose Johnson; he was efficient and ruthless, but lacked that extra layer of consciousness which would ever make the man question an order.

"On my way. Out," replied Taylor. His intention was not to upset or injure the president in any way, and his orders were specific; the president was to be treated with the respect due his office. They needed him to legitimize their coup and to be the face of the new direction their country was heading in, whether he liked it or not. Demonstrating that they could reduce one of the biggest cities in on the continent, in the world in fact, to chaos, was a sharp axe to hold over a man's neck.

Taylor stalked into the luxurious suite of rooms which had been turned into an isolation cell, nodded to Johnson and the other soldier, dismissing them.

"Sir," he said, saluting, "you wanted to see me?" The man in front of him, red-faced as though the anger he was holding in would not stay shuttered up for long, regarded him.

"Taylor," he said acidly, not so much remembering the man as reading his name from the uniform shirt, "just how long do you think this little charade will go on?" he asked him, taking the same approach as when they had first spoken.

"Sir, we need to keep you safe until morning. Then you can talk to my commanding officer—" Taylor said before being savagely cut off.

"*I* am your goddamned commanding officer, you son of a bitch," the president snarled at him through bared teeth. "You've heard the term 'Commander in Chief,' have you not?"

"Yes, sir, I have," Taylor said, still stood to attention and showing the respect the man's position demanded, even if he had no respect for the man himself. He said nothing more, but turned and left the room offering another nod to the soldiers outside the door.

"This is *treason*, goddammit!" erupted the president at his retreating back.

"Nobody in or out, and you have my permission to restrain him if he gets outta line," he told Johnson. "Just don't leave any visible injuries," he added as he walked away, thinking of the press conference the president would be holding the following day.

Friday 9:38 p.m. - 17th Precinct, NYC

Jake closed his eyes, knowing he was about to die. The gunshot he heard didn't sound right, nor did he feel any pain or impact from the bullet. A second and third shot rang out, interspersed with the rapid coughing sound of the weapon aimed at him. Only with the absence of his painful death did it occur to Jake that the unsuppressed shots could not have come from the silenced assault rifle which had promised his death only a second before. His brain eventually registered that the shots sounded just like those from his own gun, and he only opened an eye when the sound of a body slumping to the street made him jolt.

The shooter, slightly bigger than the first but dressed in dark clothing carrying a similar backpack, lay dead in front of him. Clearly dead, unlike the one he had shot, because he hadn't shot his suspect in the face and left a gruesome hole where the nose had been. Just as he reached out an instinctive hand to check for a pulse, an autonomous reaction he made in shock as missing a part of your brain to a bullet nearly always resulted in death, another sound grabbed his attention.

"Motherf-uuuugh ..." came a hissing grunt from in the street.

Rising back into action, Jake scanned the street and laid eyes on his worst nightmare. He threw himself down next to a man dressed as he was, of roughly the same age, and in obvious agony.

"Where are you hit?" Jake asked as he tried to roll the cop onto his back to see the wound.

"Groin," the man growled through gritted teeth and eyes screwed tightly shut, "and in the vest."

Jake pulled up his uniform shirt to see that the shooter's burst had raked across at gut level and the rounds had caught the bottom of his vest, but one lucky round had dropped and impacted low on his hip.

"Keep pressure on it," Jake told him, as the man opened one eye to look at him.

"One-Three?" he gasped, seeing the metal badges on Jake's uniform collar. "The hell are you doing up here?" he asked, meaning that he wouldn't often see a member of the 13th precinct in his native One-Seven.

"Chased the shooters," he told him, adding, "one killed, one unconscious."

"Good," gasped the wounded cop.

"Look, we need to get you inside and get a bus," Jake told him, not knowing how he would do that when there was no cell coverage, no phone lines, and no radio to use to call for an ambulance. "Secure them," the cop said, fluttering a weak hand toward the shooters. Jake glanced in that direction, and only saw one.

"Fuck!" he cursed aloud, releasing the pressure on the bullet wound and drawing his gun again. He stalked three paces forwards, seeing the one he had bashed in the face crawling on the sidewalk. No warnings, no verbal commands to comply, Jake stepped over and kicked the shooter full in the ribs before dropping a knee into his back and hauling hands to his back where he applied the cuffs far tighter than he would with any normal suspect. The gasp which came from under the ski mask gave him pause, and he pulled it off to see the angry, defiant, and bloodied face of a woman. Before he could say anything, she spat at him, and tried to flip on her back to use her feet as weapons. Jake stepped quickly back and raised his gun at her.

She didn't seem to care, pulling back her foot and spinning on her back to deliver a brutal stamp at his knees intent on crippling him. He stepped aside, drew back his own boot, and kicked her in the chest like he was sending up a field goal.

He had gained the desired effect, and her attempts to fight back stopped. He dragged her back toward his wounded colleague, thinking that treating a suspect like he just had and brutalizing them in cuffs, would probably cost him his badge and his life's ambition on any other day.

He found the cop weak and pale, his lips fluttering as he tried to speak. Looking up and around for the nearest refuge, Jake saw the lights of the Waldorf up ahead.

~

Sebastian had regained his composure and got all the guests upstairs or back to their rooms, amidst ridiculous questions of such ludicrous natures as to warrant an unkind response.

"No sir, I don't know if the cable TV is working. No madam, I do not think the kitchens will be providing room service at this time," he said calmly, even though he wanted to yell at them all to stop being so self-centered and entitled for five minutes and do as they were goddamned told. He doubted if many of them fully understood the neck-deep level of shit they were in now, and how surviving the night was not a guaranteed prospect at this time.

He turned to find Cal and Louise still with him. "You two need to get upstairs too, please." Cal opened his mouth to protest but Sebastian cut him off. "Cal, you're pretty beat up. You need to rest, hell you probably need to spend at least a night in hospital, but something tells me that's not going to happen."

Cal went to speak again but another sound cut him off.

"NYPD!" came the familiar but unexpected shout. All eyes turned to the street to see Jake, sweating, and breathing hard, outside the glass front with another cop over one shoulder in a fireman's carry and a dark shape dragging on the ground in his right hand.

"Jake?" Cal said as Sebastian moved forwards to open the bolts and let him in.

"Help Tromans," he gasped, short of breath. He knew only three things about the now-unconscious brother he carried; he knew he was a cop from the 17th precinct as dictated by the numbers on his collar, he knew he was called Tromans thanks to the name badge on his chest, and he was badly hurt—probably dying.

Sebastian lifted the burden off Jake, carrying the man further inside the lobby and laying him down as he called out the names of staff to help him. Cal helped Jake drag his other burden inside, his shock registering with a single curse word.

"What the hell happened?" Louise asked.

Jake dropped to his knees, exhausted at having carried the dead weight of two people the short distance. "Shooters. Terrorists probably. One is dead and this one's unconscious. The other one got Tromans just as he got him. I need to get back out there ..." he said, climbing to his feet and reapplying the handcuffs to the unconscious woman to lock her arms around a pillar.

"Are you joking?" Cal said, putting a hand on his shoulder.

"The other one. I need to bring him in. His equipment ..." Jake gasped in between deep breaths as he sucked in oxygen.

"I'm coming with you," Cal told him, forgetting his own physical state in worry that Jake would go back out alone.

"Okay," Jake said surprising Cal by not arguing. "Stay close and do as I say. It's not far."

As they left, Louise picked up the large pistol from where Sebastian had left it while tending to Tromans. She stood guard by the door with the nervous remaining members of the paid security staff.

Three minutes later, Jake appeared at the door with his gun in both hands and eyes darting everywhere. Screams and shouts erupted in the street outside and the flickering orange light told

Louise there was a fire nearby. Cal dragged in a body dressed in dark clothing and streaking blood from where the head scraped along the ground. The lobby was locked up, and the lights dimmed to leave the security guards watching the glass front. Jake's first priority was Tromans, and he walked over to see that his uniform had been cut away and gauze was being packed onto the hole in his hip. His skin looked gray.

Sebastian looked up at Jake and shook his head slightly before returning his attention to the wound. Jake swallowed, and walked back to his two suspects; one dead and one unconscious.

"Tromans is *likely* …" he told Cal and Louise, confusing them. Neither knew what he meant, and it pained him to explain it. "Likely to die from his injuries," he told them. He pushed past the devastating news and knelt by the dead suspect. He peeled off the face mask, showing the gore of where the bullet had made his features seem less human. Stripping off his backpack he emptied the contents and sat back on his boots with his mouth wide open.

The backpack contained a stack of spare magazines which he laid out next to the gun, a bullpup design none of them had ever seen anything like before. Its fat, oversized barrel had a built-in suppressor, and a red-tinted holographic sight sat above the carry handle.

He found knives and a pistol on the body, as well as a dozen grenades in the bag, but no comms devices, no orders, and nothing to say who they were. There was a map of the city which Jake unfolded and smoothed down, wiping blood across it as he did. There were targets marked, and writing pointing to the targets in lettering he couldn't read.

"Is that, Chinese?" Louise asked.

"I don't know. Could be," Jake answered. "Or Korean?"

"What the fuck is going on?" Cal asked openmouthed, thinking that the world had just gotten even weirder.

"I don't know," Jake said again, "but these assholes killed at least one man and put a bullet in a cop. These sure as shit aren't your regular gun thugs," he added.

That much was obvious. The weapons bore no trademarks, no manufacturer's details, and didn't register in Jake's mind even though he had been trained and had studied to learn the caliber, capacity, and capabilities of weapons. He popped a round out of one of the magazines and studied the bullet with a furrowed brow, not having seen a round of that size and makeup before.

That certainly isn't American-made, he told himself. Looking at the metallic tubes with the obvious trappings of a grenade, he studied the cylinders to see if he could make out any legend. Nothing. He had never seen a grenade without warnings or markings showing what it was; the thing in his hand could be smoke or an incendiary. He put it down carefully, then replaced the contents of the bag before zipping it all up tightly. A shout from behind followed by the sound of a woman crying made the three of them turn.

Tromans had gone.

Jake rose uncertainly, walked slowly toward the blood-soaked scene, and looked down on his fellow police officer. His blue-blooded brother. The two had never met before that day, and would be unlikely to have ever met in their entire careers, but he was dead now. Jake, uncertain of what to do, carefully removed his NYPD shield and the precinct badges from the collar of his shirt, as well as his duty belt and equipment, draped the sheet which one of the hotel staff had brought over his body, and laid the badges on top. He rested his duty belt over one shoulder and turned.

He froze, eyes wide, looking past Cal and Louise. The two slowly turned their heads to look in the direction he was staring, and found themselves looking into the murderous eyes of the handcuffed and broken-nosed woman, now awake and pulling one bloody hand free of the restraints.

Cal, as useless as he had felt when the gang had robbed the hotel, acted on instinct. He was the closest person to the now escaped prisoner, and he threw himself at her with an animalistic bellow of rage, but without any regard for his safety or thought for his next move. He was vaguely aware of screams behind him, unsure if it was Louise or someone else, but he was sure it wasn't the lithe assassin he tried to rush. She was cold, collected, and much faster than him.

She let his bull-rush come, turned her body slightly to divert the force of his attack and rolled him over her hip. As he felt himself losing the control and initiative of his attack, he was stuck once again by feeling useless and incompetent. She had grabbed one of his wrists as he rolled past her, which was now pulled tight as she painfully dragged his arm up straight. Cal's eyes went wide as he saw her raise her right foot to smash down on his arm and he knew it was going to get horribly broken. He thought about closing his eyes, but couldn't tear his gaze away from the look of bloodthirsty glee on her face.

A flash and an echoing bang reverberated around the lobby, making his damaged and sensitive ears ring again. At the same time his attacker's upper body convulsed; her left shoulder pitched backwards with the momentum of the round which had struck her vest. Before she regained her composure and finished him, another flash and bang erupted from a different direction.

Cal blinked and gasped as blood fountained on his face, misty at first but coming thicker quickly. It was hot, and tasted metallic in his mouth. Between blinks of his eyes, he could see her face. Could see it had changed from ruthless anger to unregistered shock, but no pain.

She didn't waver on her feet or fall to her knees dramatically like in the movies, but was carried forwards by the momentum of the bullet to land face down heavily on Cal like a felled tree. Blood gushed out of the wound on the side of her skull to pulse in great gouts onto Cal's chest. Scrabbling to get free of the butcher's scene on top of him, he managed to wriggle out from underneath her body and wipe at his face.

Looking up through a gulp of fresh air, he first saw Jake still holding his weapon aimed at where she had been stood. Glancing to his right, he saw Louise. Her eyes were wide with terror, but the thin trails of smoke lingering and creeping lazily upwards from the barrel of the pistol she held told him the rest. He couldn't have explained it then, but he knew from his subconscious where the shots had come from. Both had fired shots at the woman about to snap Cal's arm in half, but being the trained man of the two, Jake had fired first and hit her high in the vest, just left of center-mass. As she spun with the momentum of that first hit, the fateful trajectory of Louise's shot had resulted in the removal of part of the right side of her skull just above the ear.

Silence reigned in the lobby, as everyone exchanged looks which conveyed any number of questions. None of these questions had the chance to be put into words, as a muted flash and a rolling grumble of thunder vibrated the whole island.

BRINGER OF DEATH

The dull red light inside the command section of the Virginia class fast attack submarine lit the faces of the concerned Navy Commander. His entire crew had been on full alert for over three hours now, as a quick glance at the mission clock running next to him said. Their task, as it had been for weeks, was to patrol the waters and provide advanced warning of vessels moving in unexpected patterns outside of the South American and Caribbean shipping lanes. They were the eyes, or more appropriately the ears, which gave the US Navy and Coastguard forces the much-appreciated heads up.

This elusive radar contact, the one which had disturbed his meal and now made him unable to shake off a sense of dread, had evaded his boat for far too long. His XO, executive officer, tried again to reassure the commander of the sub that it was nothing to worry over.

"Sir, I still believe this was a ghost," he said for the third time, a hint of annoyance creeping into his voice.

"This wasn't a ghost," the commander said, meaning that the ping they had detected and been searching for these last hours was not a malfunction in their sensor equipment. The signal he had seen before it disappeared was big, too big to be a pod of whales or some sonar echo to be ignored. He had an impending sense of dread that his crew had accidentally detected something malevolent and dangerous. His mind wandered from the displays to imagine a hidden killer sensing that they had been detected. If he were that imaginary shrouded hunter, he would have slowed to a dead crawl and dropped low to sneak past the American boat above, pinging sonar like a game of Marco Polo played in the pitch-black depths. Eventually he had to accept that his paranoia was putting the crew on edge.

"Stand down," he called to the command section suddenly, reassuring himself that no submarine in the known world could have avoided their sensor array for that long and only be glimpsed partially once.

Saturday 10:13 a.m. Local Time, Beijing

A change of shift happened effectively in phases as first the supervision then the operators were replaced in small groups. Only the two people in their anonymous dark suits remained from the collective which had first watched events unfold in New York.

Men in stiff uniforms adorned with medals came and went, shooting cautious glances in the direction of the secretive pair.

They had not been summoned or addressed, so the military men left the suits to their own devices.

The woman glanced to her left, seeing the telltale glow of a burning cigarette end showing in the darker shadows. Her gaze lingered for a moment, knowing that the older man would be able to make out her features as she was bathed in dull light from the screens, but was unable to see his. She wanted to ask if it was time, if the tension could be broken and they could unleash the incredible might of the People's Republic on their western enemies, but to ask would be to show a weakness of character that she had fought for years to hide from everyone. She was every part the stone-cold operator that he was, but she was a generation younger and had plans to rise further than she already had. Not a single woman in the country outranked her. She was at the apex of her gender amongst 1.3 billion people, and still she intended to rise higher. Everywhere she went she could sense, almost *taste*, the shame of high-ranking officials having to obey her commands. Her country had conscripted female soldiers for generations, for millennia even, but today she felt that female soldiers were a gimmick and weren't taken seriously. Her dedication and aptitude had smashed those molds, and her recruitment into the Ministry of State Security had been, for her, an inevitability.

She cast her eyes back at the screens, seeing mixed reports of empty streets shown alongside fires and looting.

"Now," said the voice simply from the shadows next to her.

She said nothing, but straightened and smoothed down the dark skirt of her dark suit. She walked forward to stand on the raised dais behind the ranks of busily working analysts. After buttoning the jacket over her plain blouse, she lit another cigarette, and steadied herself. She was about to give the order, albeit by proxy, for the biggest military decision in modern history.

She took a long drag from her cigarette, held it, then let it out slowly. "Begin the operation," she announced, adding only slightly more information than the head of State Security had given her. Everyone there knew their role, everyone was read in on the plans—those parts which they were cleared to know at least—but then again if they were in that room then they already knew what China had done to the United States, and more importantly what they were about to do.

~

Captain Wayne Grant, formerly of the United States Air Force, stood up and smoothed his own expensive suit in a control room thousands of miles away from Beijing. He was five decks below sea level on the newest vessel of the People's Liberation Army Navy's fleet. The Type 002A carrier, only the second carrier not to have been bought from another country as a hand-me-down, was shiny and new. Although only two thirds the size of the floating cities the US had put to sea which Grant had spent much of his time aboard, this Chinese carrier boasted an efficient crew and a full complement of the J-15 *Flying Sharks*.

Although trusted, and only sometimes afforded a chaperone which he suspected was more of a bodyguard, Grant had the run of the place. He wore no uniform, and was exquisitely tailored at the expense of his new masters. It seemed to him that his lack of uniform in any military setting was a uniform in itself, and he found that even senior ranks were wary of his presence.

In the six years since he had been declared officially dead by his country after punching out from the cockpit of his F-22 Raptor, he had experienced a great many new things. The irony of it kicked him square in the gut. Despite his years of training and being at the controls of a cutting-edge weapon of destruction, he'd still ended up being shot down by a goat-herder using a shoulder-mounted weapon. A weapon that his own country had provided a generation before. After that, he had been beaten and imprisoned, but never once used as propaganda material despite being trained to expect the kind of internet home video that every citizen fears seeing a loved one appear on. Nobody cut off his head, nobody informed the United States government of his capture, and they had simply given up looking for him. Not that Grant had any family left back home to scour the internet for videos of his demise by beheading.

It took almost a year, during which time he had been questioned but otherwise mostly ignored, but he had found himself being transported long distances by car, boat, and aircraft until he found himself on a small island being treated by Chinese medical staff as though he were in some expensive rehab clinic for the wealthy and secretive one percenters. He tried to run, and they simply let him. He soon found that the island was small, so small that he ran from one side to the other fearing pursuit, and that there were no means by which he could transport himself off. With ocean on all sides as far as he could see, he walked back to the clinic and accepted the treatment on offer, along with a refreshing, cold beer.

His loyalty had been stretched, and apparently hadn't been that firm to begin with, because he willingly accepted the offer to become a Chinese citizen and join the Ministry of State Security as an advisor to the People's Army. He was treated like a general everywhere he went, and now he was officially advising the officers overseeing the air operations of the next phase of their plan. He had no need to give orders, as he found the Chinese beyond reproach when it came to the efficiency of their military operations. He was there to simply advise if the commanders needed their own home-grown American to ask what their opposition was thinking and doing.

In his heart, he knew he had been turned. He knew that the psychological pressure and careful treatment had led to him feeling aggrieved with the country of his birth and who he served, but if he was honest, he liked his new life. Fighter pilots by their very nature are showboats, and he never lacked for respect or admiration. And he certainly never lacked for attractive women around him, even if he was sure they were now paid to keep him company.

Knowing all this, he was still okay with it. Happy, in fact.

Hearing the commands given and feeling the familiar vibrations as the cargo lifts began their slow grind to bring aircraft to the flight deck, he listened to the orders given and heard the command to launch the H-9s.

That made him smile, despite the purpose of the order. The H-9 had been developed in secret, and Grant had even played some small part in the final design tweaks. It was a cutting edge, lightweight, long-range stealth bomber which the rest of the world hadn't yet seen. It was small enough to take off and land from a carrier, carried an intense payload, and flew so high that the bombs would fall on their targets without the targets ever even knowing about it. The munitions were a next-generation hybrid of drone technology and old-school bomb drops. The pilot, and in Grant's obvious view no machine could ever replace a real person at the controls of a plane, could fly so high as to never be at risk of attack and drop his payload somewhere vaguely in the vicinity of the target. The system was ingenious, and, he was told, actually inspired by a cult sci-fi film made in America.

The payload consisted of a single dart-like bomb no bigger than a football. That was guided by the co-pilot by drone feed on a screen to the desired target, and then the pilot would release the rest of the bombs. They only had to make one pass high overhead, drop their targeting ordnance, then effectively toss everything else out of the window because the bombs then flew themselves directly onto the target to the desired spread pattern, and would either delay detonation for maximum penetration or could airburst and deploy over the head of anywhere. He knew, as did the senior officers onboard and the pilots themselves, that each plane carried only two guidance systems and two pieces of ordnance each on their first bombing run. He also knew that what they carried similarly hadn't been seen by the rest of the world before.

Their vastly improved range meant that they could fly undetected for almost the range of any Inter-Continental Ballistic Missile, or ICBM, and fly home again, meaning that the carrier was even now still in international waters. The US military were obviously aware that a Chinese carrier group were heading for their waters, but the nominal warning had been given that they were heading around the southern part of the continent to eventually visit the Chinese-built port in Cuba. No doubt the strength of the *escort* they would receive would be a huge show of strength, but that was never going to happen. Their eastern seaboard operations were another matter, and Grant suspected that he knew more about them than even the captain of the carrier he was on.

"I'm going up," he told his aides in Mandarin, a language he had surprisingly taken to with ease, and followed the young sailor assigned to them as a guide. They climbed the ladders to the glass circle of the flight control deck, high above the tarmac below, and watched in awe as the sleek birds rose from the depths. Preflight checks were quick, far quicker than he had experienced in his own flying career, and he even smiled as, one by one, the four H-9s took off from the ski ramp beside the prow of the ship and dropped slightly before powering away almost vertically to reach the thin air on the edge of space.

Friday 11:46 p.m. – Washington, D.C.

"Sir! Major!" Johnson's voice said over the squad radio, full of uncharacteristic panic.

"On my way," Taylor answered, nodding to his captain and senior sergeant to follow him as he set off for the president's suite at a run. Bursting through the ornate double doors, Taylor saw Johnson fighting to control the president on the thick rug as the other soldier lay unconscious and bleeding next to a heavy bust of a man who had held the same office in the past. The president himself was raging, fighting against Johnson's grip like a wounded bull, and all the time shouting abuse and curses at them.

"SIR!" barked Taylor, trying and failing to gain the attention of the man. Johnson was no small man, nor was he unaccustomed to fighting, but the intensity in the struggles of the President made him sweat and suck in breath just to hold him down.

"You sons of bitches," he bawled, his words contorted by the plush pile of the rug his face was pushed into. "You fucking traitors. You've destroyed our country!"

This made Taylor stop. They had hardly destroyed their country, hell they had barely destroyed anything but a handful of buildings at worst, but the tears in the eyes of the man told him that this was something worse.

"Sir," Anderson said behind him, his voice so deathly hollow and subdued that Taylor dreaded turning around to look at him. He did, and followed the outstretched finger of his second-in-command to the TV screen and the unbelievable picture it showed.

The ticker-tape read "Los Angeles Disaster," and the picture showed something none of them would have ever wanted to see in their lives. It wasn't the mushroom cloud image that everyone recognized from Hiroshima, but something so similar and exponentially worse that nobody spoke. The image was fleeting, and soon replaced by another scene; similar but different and appeared to be coming live from the window of a plane many miles from the explosion. Twice more the image switched.

"LA," said Anderson. "San Francisco. Seattle. Vegas."

Nobody could manage a word in response, until the grunting from the president abated. Johnson had released him and stood, walking straight up to Taylor's face where he looked angrily into his eyes. Taylor vaguely recalled that Johnson came from Vegas, or California at least, but somewhere that the bombs had just fallen.

"Did we do this?" he snarled angrily in his commanding officer's face.

"No," Taylor said, his voice barely above a whisper, but even as he spoke the screen switched again to show another explosion, this one recent.

"Airburst," Anderson said simply in the same hollow voice he had used before. Taylor looked at the screen, this time showing Portland and what appeared to be a recent nuclear detonation just above the Earth and directly over the city. The human casualties he calculated off the top of his head were already the single largest loss of life in the history of mankind. He turned to the president to explain, to plead with him to understand that this wasn't their doing, but he was gone. Putting one boot in front of the other to follow, he felt a vibration, then it felt as though a gale were blowing through the house itself, then his world went white and blinked out in an instant.

~

The five missiles fired from the protruding hump of the nuclear-powered submarine shot straight upwards, then arced off in different directions as the submarine slipped back below the surface. The new design, as with the H-9 bombers, was as yet unseen by the rest of the world and had been developed in total secret at off-shore shipyards under cover to keep the prying eyes of the American satellites away. The shimmering, advanced camouflage skin of the sleek underwater killer had evaded the laughable efforts of the Americans as they sailed in circles effectively shouting to see if anyone answered. The crew of the submarine had simply stopped dead in the water and allowed themselves to sink slowly and then continue at a lower depth until well out of range of the shouts of their searchers.

It was the only one of its design, the Type 096A, and was effectively the prototype which had been put to work early. It could only carry a small payload of five missiles, and those were not the standard missiles the rest of the world expected. The payload was only four megatons, the same size as the ones currently dropping on the west coast of the United States, but with a twelve-thousand kilometer range the sub could safely pop up in the Atlantic, fire its ordnance, and slip away again.

Those five JL-4A SLBMs, or submarine-launched ballistic missiles, now streaked inland at six times the speed of sound. One headed for Fort Bragg in North Carolina, where over fifty thousand active service men and women were based. The remainder, instead of the tactical target selection of the first, streaked toward population centers. Streaked, with the exception of one which had an undetected malfunction in the solid fuel engine, making it splutter along at half its top speed.

Florida was the first to suffer the most recent attack in the devastating flurry of airburst nuclear weaponry, and most of the inhabitants of that spit of land never even had the opportunity to wake and know what killed them. As the Chinese submarine slipped away off the east coast, Florida had been wiped out inside of seven minutes. Had the malfunctioning missiles been aimed there, the course of the sudden and unannounced war would have been drastically altered.

Washington D.C., already on edge due to the presidential lockdown situation which had been ongoing for a few hours, had the added benefit that many people were still awake. Many were even still out, wrapped up against the cool air and held back behind police cordons with a view of the Capitol, and many couldn't resist the pull of looking toward the sudden flash of bright light. Those who did were blinded instantly, as the worst and brightest firework display they would ever see erupted over the skies of the capital. After the flash came the heat; the intense, unfathomable heat which incinerated anyone close enough to the explosion like they were nothing but steam in a hurricane. With the flash, the heat, and the boiling cloud floating high above the seat of power for the country, came the shockwave. From a distance, it would look as though heavy smoke rolled out over the ground, but up close it would be the worst destruction and devastation ever dreamt possible by man.

Entire buildings, cars, buses, crowds of people; all of them were wiped out in an instant. Erased from the face of the earth like insignificant insects facing the might of a power they could never even begin to understand. The destruction was unimaginable, unending, and unstoppable. The White House ceased to exist, as did the capitol building. Almost two hundred and thirty years of political control erased in an instant.

GO TO HELL

Cal stopped talking to Louise when Jake was taking a turn at consoling her. He half listened to the young cop giving advice which he himself had never needed until very recently. He heard the words coming from a man he must have at least a decade on, and although he knew they were well intended, he also suspected they may sound hollow to others too.

~

High over their heads and thousands of miles to their north west, screaming south east at a little over eight thousand miles an hour, tore five ABMs, anti-ballistic missiles, fired in automatic response from a US base in Alaska. Because the distance of the launches was far shorter than expected, less than one hundred miles off the east coast, the Movement missiles devised for the mid-course intercepts were pointless to launch, instead they relied on the new system designed and tested in secret.

The Chinese weren't the only world power to have unleashed new technology that night, and when the word was given to launch five of the thirty-six Seeker 6 missiles the United States had at their disposal, just about everyone held their breath. Testing had proven to be 100 percent effective, but they were on the back foot. The nukes detonated on the west coast weren't missile-borne, but the signatures which set alarms screaming from the Atlantic near Florida were in play.

Lieutenant Colonel Andy Gilbert stood at ease as he watched the signatures on the big screen split apart and head in different directions.

"Acquire targets," he called out to his control room, "prepare to fire five Seekers."

"Targets acquired," came a calm response, "fire on your mark."

"Fire," said Gilbert instantly with no trace of hesitation, feeling the facility shake with the combined force of five rockets capable of almost Mach-9 erupting into the sky far above them.

The threat had first come from the Soviet Union, and the facility he stood in was built as a direct response to that threat of mutually assured destruction. The United States had no desire to agree to be destroyed and, just as every other country in possession of nuclear warheads, began another arms race with more intensity than the space race to develop the most effective intercept missiles. These next generation missiles were designed with another purpose, rather than another tool in the box for two heavyweights to slug it out. The threat they feared more today was a short-range attack, or a nuclear or chemical or biological attack coming in by plane. The Seekers were designed to outrun everything known to fly, and instead of carrying a warhead, it relied on kinetic energy to displace the attack.

The program started way back in the eighties and was intended for short range use as tank busters, but the project was subsequently cancelled. It was quietly reinvented in the windowless meeting rooms of government buildings, using specialists in different fields like solid-fuel propulsion and electronic guidance systems all working in information silos and never getting together until the prototypes were ready.

"Target analysis," Gilbert called out. "Intercept percentage."

"Missile trajectory indicates Florida, Nashville, D.C., Boston, or New York. Last missile is a slow-mover and indicates ..." The analyst paused, trying to search the digital map along the projected line of the missile's path for a target. Gilbert didn't snap at the woman, didn't allow his fear and nerves to dictate how he treated his team. He permitted her a few seconds.

"Sir, based on trajectory I believe it could be heading for Pittsburgh," she said finally.

"Could be?" Gilbert asked, his need for certainty greater than ever.

"Sir, trajectory is off for direct line, but no other major population center is in the path," she answered. Before Gilbert could ruminate on that another analyst called out with panic in their voice.

"*Impact!* Detonation over Florida," he squealed in panic. Gilbert fully expected that this would happen. He couldn't do the complex calculations in his head with other things happening in quick time, but he knew that their missiles couldn't cover the short distance that the first missile had covered in a matter of seconds.

"Understood," he said coolly, swallowing. "Intercept percentage," he said again.

"Sir," the female analyst again, "slower moving missile at one hundred per cent, D.C. thirty-eight percent."

"And the others?" Gilbert asked, the note of his voice changing slightly as he absorbed the majority likelihood that their capital would be annihilated in minutes.

"Looks like Boston, sir." A pause. "Negative outcome. Twenty-one per cent intercept chance. Incoming missiles are accelerating faster than we anticipated."

"*Impact!*" shouted the analyst. "It's … it's D.C. sir …"

"Understood," Gilbert said again in a deadpan voice, staring at the screen resolutely.

"*Impact!*" shouted the excitable analyst again. "North of Fayetteville," he said, scanning a map for the target.

"Fort Bragg," Gilbert said, not needing a map to know what was just to the north west of the city. Gilbert waited, his hands clasped together and his breathing rapid as he watched the illuminated legends creep across the screen. The missile heading for Boston blinked out, and was followed by another impact report. Gilbert barely heard it, but acknowledged it all the same. He was reminded of the serenity prayer; he had to accept the things he could not change, he had used courage to change, or at least try to change, the things he could, and now he was learning the wisdom to tell the difference.

"Intercept!" screamed the analyst. "Remaining missile taken down near Atlanta."

The control room cheered as one, not realizing the devastation they had just suffered, or simply not fully understanding it yet. Inside of a few tense minutes they had lost one of their biggest military bases, two cities with millions of casualties, and their capital. Gilbert stayed in the position he was stood in, rooted to the spot and fighting to keep himself calm.

And the attack would go, for now at least, unanswered. Because there was nobody left alive with the authority to launch a counterstrike.

The Movement, the treasonous fools, had ensured that, unwittingly, by securing the president and making him the perfect sitting duck.

~

Just as Jake was trying to emulate the easy manner of command that he had seen in others, a flash like lightning seared across the windows. It was like lightning, but at the same time it couldn't be because the flash lingered instead of plunging the sky back into darkness. As the flash began to wane, a rumbling of something far away hit them as though they were on the very edge on a small earthquake.

Some people didn't notice it, others did and began to ask questions. Jake, Cal, and Sebastian all exchanged looks.

"Sir," Jake asked Sebastian. "Do you have roof access here?"

"Yes," he replied as he unclipped his own swipe card, "service elevator to the top."

Jake said nothing but glanced to Cal. His eyes said, *You coming?* and Cal nodded. He looked to Sebastian, then to Louise, and the concierge nodded back. Inside of a second, the three men had communicated a great deal without saying a word.

Cal limped alongside Jake who swiped the card over the elevator controls. The doors opened straight away and the two men entered the small space, both unbeknownst to the other saying a silent prayer that the generator power held up. Riding upwards fast in the undecorated space in stark contrast to the decadence of the guest's elevator, neither said a word. It creaked to a stop and the two walked out, still in silence. They scanned the horizon until Jake's sharp intake of breath made Cal spin around.

There, in the very furthest reaches of his vision to their north east, was a glowing orb. Neither man could see it clearly, and neither knew what it was with any certainty.

But both knew that it wasn't good.

~

Moments after the cop had got into the elevator with Cal, Sebastian was leading Louise through to the comfortable seats further inside the lobby. As he was doing so, a shout from the lounge made him divert.

"I got something," shouted an excited voice, as the volume of a TV screen grew louder. "Oh, Jesus ..."

On the screen, on some obscure news channel nobody had heard of, was the obvious devastation and recognizable profile of a nuclear detonation.

"Where is that?" shouted a guest. "Is that the west coast?"

"That's LA," responded a voice full of dreadful certainty.

"Everybody quiet!" snapped Sebastian as he sat the shocked Louise down in a chair. "Please, turn that up."

"...*confirmed reports of between six and ten nuclear explosions in the United States,*" said the anchor's strained voice. Sebastian didn't hear any more as the gathering of guests who had refused to go back to their rooms erupted with gasps and shouted curses and questions.

Just then Jake and Cal returned to the ground floor and followed the source of the noise. As they rounded the corner into the lounge, both saw the iconic and unmistakable profile of a mushroom cloud, only this one was hanging over the earth instead of rising up from it. Both then knew, with absolute and utter horrified certainty, what the glow they had seen from the roof was.

"Boston," Jake said quietly, making Cal's mouth open. Between the report on TV and the information he had gathered with his own eyes, he put together the information in the only way it could logically go. East and west coast alike, the USA was being bombed by nukes.

"It's the Russians, it has to be," shouted an old man in a tuxedo, angrily shaking off the restraining arm of his wife and personally reliving the cold war.

"What the hell are you doing about this?" screamed a woman with tear-streaked makeup running down her face. She directed this at Jake, as though his membership of the NYPD had made him the keeper of international relations and that he was somehow solely responsible for this. He knew it was fear transference; people when they panic look for the nearest uniform, the nearest authority figure, and either plead for help or blame them personally.

"Okay everyone, let's all just calm down for a minute," he said, holding up both hands to try and restore order to the small group. This only had the desired effect of making people shout louder and advance on him like a pack of hungry animals. The mob fragmented between the majority going after Jake and demanding he do something, and a smaller group who had singled out an Arab businessman in a perfectly cut shiny suit.

Cal didn't see this, he was advancing himself toward the TV screen, reading the text scrolling across the bottom.

Los Angeles, San Francisco. Seattle. Vegas. Portland. North Carolina. Florida, and now Boston.

"How far away is Boston from here?" he asked nobody in particular.

"Couple hundred miles, straight line. Maybe less," Sebastian said behind his shoulder.

"Prevailing wind?" Cal shot back.

"This way, more or less," Sebastian answered, grasping the point immediately. "We need to move west or north. Fast."

They turned, and Cal squatted down in front of Louise. He held her hand, seeing that she was coming out of the other end of whatever shock she had fallen into. Cal told her the country was under attack, and that they had to go. Now.

"My bag," she said. "I need my bag."

Cal glanced between her and the mob yelling at Jake. He saw that the young cop had taken a step backwards, then bladed his stance and placed a hand on his right hip; the classic stance for facing a threat and gently reminding everyone there that he had a gun. He had three actually, given that he still had Troman's duty belt over one shoulder and his off-duty weapon in the rig under his left arm, but his instinctive stance to rely on his service weapon was ingrained. Cal heard him shouting at the others to stay back. He knew just by looking that the situation would not end well. Wordlessly he took the chrome semi-automatic from the waist of his jeans after he had retrieved it from Louise's grasp, and went to stand beside the beleaguered NYPD officer.

The change in odds served to quiet some, whilst the others were snapped from the moment by Cal's interruption and recognized that their own behavior was simply not acceptable.

"Enough! Everybody, listen to me!" came an authoritative shout from behind the group. Almost as one, heads turned to see Sebastian stood on a polished mahogany table with his arms out wide. "The United States is under attack." He paused for the rising noise level to react to his repetition of the obvious.

"It's the fucking Al-Qaeda," a voice shouted, the owner of which pointed a finger at the terrified businessman.

"Don't be so bloody ignorant," snapped Cal loudly. "For one, Al-Qaeda barely even exists anymore and you're just being bigoted, and two, why would *he* have anything to do with it?"

"Enough!" said Sebastian again, raising his voice but still not quite lowering himself to shout. "We all need to evacuate the city and head west. We have probably a day before the fallout reaches New York so again, I urge you to leave."

"How do you know?" shouted a man in a suit.

"I don't," Sebastian answered equably, "but I doubt staying in the city is the right thing to do, so I think we should try and leave. How you do this is up to you. Thank you."

With that he skipped down from the table and undid his tie, symbolically taking himself away from his duty to ensure everyone visiting the hotel was thoroughly cared for. People milled around, uncertain of what to do without instruction. Sebastian strode through the crowd, ignoring all the shouts and pleas to help them. Glancing back, he caught Cal's eye, then Jake's. Cal involuntarily stepped forward to follow before he remembered Louise and turned back for her. She was already on her feet, walking toward him with some sparkle back in her eyes.

"It's all on the coast," she said, "we need to go inland."

"What?" Cal said, slightly behind her logic.

"I saw it on the news," she said looking straight at him. "All those bombs dropped on the coast, so we need to head inland away from them. I need to go home."

That was a concept Cal understood perfectly, only he knew now with utter certainty that he would probably never go home, even if he found an airport with something capable of crossing the Atlantic that would take him. He misunderstood her point in its entirety, however, because her need to get home wasn't for need of a feeling of safety, but because she knew they would be far safer there than anywhere else.

Louise went to activate the elevator to retrieve her bag, but as she was waiting a noise erupted in the lobby. A series of bangs and flashes echoed throughout the ground floor, followed by strange coughing noises.

And then screams.

She ran back in, Jake and Cal appearing at her side with guns in hand.

"There a back way out?" Jake asked over his shoulder as they retreated from the noise ahead.

"Yes. Through the kitchen. The delivery entrance," Sebastian said, walking with them and snatching up the plain black backpacks that Jake was pointing at. He handed one to Cal, which Louise took from him and strapped on.

"Go," Jake said, hanging back slightly to cover them as the last man out.

Sebastian led the way through the kitchens, turning left and right as the head of the snake escaping the fire.

"I'm assuming a car is out of the question?" Sebastian shouted back.

"It'll be gridlock," replied Jake confidently. "We need to go on foot, head through Central Park and cross the Hudson somehow."

"Shit!" cursed Sebastian, surprising them all and stopping in his tracks.

"What?" Louise asked before any of the others could.

"The keys to my boat," he said. "They're on the bunch in my coat pocket," he said, looking forlornly back the way they had come. As if on cue, a door behind them banged open and shouts in Mandarin could be heard echoing toward them.

"I need my bag," Louise said, her eyes suddenly wide and her voice distant and desperate.

"You'll have to leave it—" Cal began to say before she cut him off.

"I need my *bag*!" she said more loudly, on the verge of tears as the shouts grew louder behind them.

"No time, go, go, go," Jake whispered, urging them all on-wards.

~

The lobby was secured with ease, and three of the team held positions of cover until the lead agent walked in. He was dressed and equipped similarly to the others: plain black equipment without labels to indicate their point of origin. He glanced down at the bodies of two of his team, a quarter of his fighting strength dead already. Chen, one of his favorites who he also knew had a sister high up in the Ministry at home, lay dead with most of the right side of her skull blown away. That was unfortunate, operationally, politically, and personally as he found himself drawn to her. He barked short orders and two of his remaining team members began to secure the bodies. Making eye contact with his partner, he nodded and the two moved off into the hotel to kill the people who did this.

~

Sebastian, now stripped of his beautifully tailored jacket and wearing a military backpack strapped on tight over his fitted shirt, led the way. He paused at the door and looked at Jake, then at the spare duty belt he carried, then back to his eyes.

"You know how to use it?" Jake asked him, receiving a curt nod in return. He handed it over and watched as the concierge strapped it on and drew the Glock, chambering a round with a smooth and practiced action after dropping the magazine to check for brass.

He silently counted down on his fingers, three, two, one, then pushed open the door and stepped clear quickly to clear the immediate area. The others pushed out behind him. Jake and Sebastian clearly knew how to handle weapons, a point which Jake made sure to ask about soon, and Cal was holding the liberated hand cannon with some form of familiarity. Only Louise was unarmed, and Jake considered giving her his Glock 26, but decided that the last thing she probably needed right then was another gun in her hand.

Sebastian led the way, checking angles, and sticking to cover like a professional. Jake put Cal and Louise in the middle—Cal because he was injured and slow, and Louise because she was, well because she was a young woman and in a semi state of shock, leaving him to secure the rear of their foot convoy. Dropping to one knee at the north end of the block, Sebastian turned to the others.

"We need to get distance from the building," he told them, full of a different kind of confidence than before. "Head for the park and up to 79th to get a boat from the basin. Agreed?"

The way he spoke told a story in itself, but for now everyone was happy to agree. Except Jake. He hesitated, holding back, and finally found his voice.

"Those people," he said, the strain evident on his face, "we can't just leave them …"

"We can, and we have to," Sebastian snapped. Cal turned to face the young cop and put his empty left hand on his shoulder.

"Jake," he said, searching for eye contact in the dark, "don't you get it? This is beyond fucked up. We need to get the hell out of here before more bombs drop. On us this time."

Jake's face fell, and Cal suspected he could see a tear roll down one cheek quickly wiped away lest it betray any sign of weakness. They were all terrified, all shocked to their very cores about how quickly normal life had turned to horror. Jake nodded, whispering, "Okay," and fighting down his pathological need to go back and help people.

There were just too many people who needed saving, and he had to prioritize. He closed his eyes for the briefest of moments and sent up a silent prayer for forgiveness. He couldn't save everyone, couldn't even realistically expect to make it back to his precinct and put himself back under the control of the NYPD command structure. He could, he assured himself, do his best to protect these civilians until they were safe. Which is what he promised himself he would do, and cross the next bridge when he came to it.

They walked together in a tightly formed line, keeping their guns hidden. The streets were in panic, as by now many people had heard of the events elsewhere in the country. Jake had lost his uniform cap in the chase north but his remaining NYPD trappings got suspicious glances from some they saw. The mixture of calm and chaos, of looting and shopkeepers remaining in their stores to protect their livelihoods, had begun to disintegrate.

Their journey took them past departments stores, some resting in the dark as though they were in hibernation and others ravaged with broken windows and stripped displays. A man careered around the corner ahead and almost thumped headfirst into Sebastian at the lead, only he stepped back and went upright against the wall to allow him to pass. His vision was obscured by the box he was holding. Amongst all the fear and chaos, amongst the world-changing events that he may or may not know about, he had chosen this precise moment to help himself to a new coffee machine.

He stumbled, saw Jake still wearing his police uniform, and completed the maneuver to fall flat on his face. The coffee machine, the now dented image of sleek plastic and shiny chrome, skidded away from his grasp as he flew back up to his feet and looked desperately left and right for inspiration and escape. He opened his mouth, stammering for a believable excuse in front of the figure of authority and enforcement. Jake saved him the trouble.

"Get the fuck out of here, asshole," he said, prompting the opportunistic looter to regard him with surprised confusion. "I said go, fuck off!"

As instructed, he went, stopping only to retrieve the coffee machine box which rattled with the unmistakable sound of broken glass as he ran. Jake holstered his gun, stripped off his uniform jacket and unstrapped his covert holster before wordlessly handing it to Cal to hold. He unbuttoned and folded his uniform shirt and handed that over for it to be stuffed into one of the liberated bags, leaving him wearing the black base layer under his vest. He strapped the rig holding his Glock 26 back on and nodded to the others.

"No judgement," he said, a plea more than a statement.

"Sensible," Sebastian said from the front of their line, eyes scanning to the front.

Ten minutes later they found the southern edge of Central Park and Jake stepped forward to take the lead.

"Central Park at night isn't as safe as they say it is, and that's on a normal day. We go straight up, toward the lake, then hit 72nd Street, okay?" They nodded in turn, Cal and Louise in total ignorance of the best way to tackle the big, dark obstacle, and followed Jake as he led the way into the inky night.

G.T.F.O.

Saturday 12:26 a.m. - Fort Campbell

The alarm sounded loudly inside the barracks. It was called a barracks, but it was bigger than some towns that the occupants had originated from. It was a city, and it bristled with more ego than many thought possible. It was an army base, but some of the elite operators under the umbrella of the 5th Special Forces Group, as well as their dedicated helicopter pilots and crews from the 160th Special Operations Aviation Regiment, also called it home. It seemed that these crazy, hard-bitten, and stone-cold operators needed pilots who were just as crazy and stone-cold as they were.

There were hospitals, training groups and schools, military police, and bomb disposal. All of which were now woken by a god-awful noise which none of them had heard in years since the training drills for a terror attack.

In the accommodation block of the 5th SFG, Captain Troy Gardner sat bolt upright to the sound of the siren and simultaneous chirping of his satellite phone. Unlike almost every other unit in the military the world over, Gardner's team of specialists operated solely within their own orbit and answered to pretty

195

much nobody. Gardner got their orders, the team worked out the mission execution as a unit, and then Gardner got the resources he asked for. They were nominally part of one of the three battalions currently based there, with one on a training exercise and two midways through foreign tours. The team, named Endeavor by their command structure, had access to the best gear and suffered none of the military discipline that other units faced daily. Few of them bothered to shave, and many wore fierce beards which could be combined with sunglasses and shemaghs to allow them to blend into obscurity in whatever country they were operating in. Physical training was a personal issue, not regimented like every other unit, and he fully expected his team to be in peak physical condition just as he was. Only a few of them were army, as ever the top-tier of special forces operators came from various sources and branches of the military on their way up, and the rivalries between Recon Marines, Army Rangers, and Navy SEALs was a daily source of amusement for them.

Troy Gardner, called Horse—short for Trojan Horse—by his team although not too often to his face, was instantly awake and fully conscious: a trait of an operator at apex predator level.

"Gardner," he said into the handset, then listened and grunted in response for a few seconds before clicking off the phone. He threw himself out of bed and into the dark fatigues folded on the chair beside his utilitarian cot. He opened the wooden locker and shrugged into his heavy vest and equipment rig. He didn't have his weapons with him, but their own armory was at least in the same block. He walked out of the door without a second glance and began to walk the corridor from one end to the other, casually kicking the doors on the left as he went then turned and walked back kicking the doors on the right. His operators appeared at their doorways, similarly shrugging themselves into their equipment.

Troy waited until all the expectant faces were assembled and gave a short speech, speaking loudly over the din.

"Word just came down," he said, "we're out of here. Clear the armory, I'll get our rides ready. Helipad in thirty." With that he turned and left, going via their armory to finish dressing himself. He gave no specific orders for who should do what, but trusted his team of nine other operators to do what needed to be done. Swiping his ID and entering a six-digit code from memory, the heavy door bleeped and swung open when he pulled it. He picked up his heavily customized FN SCAR rifle which he preferred chambered in the heavy 7.62 caliber; he hated having to scour the bodies of the enemy forces and find so many of them still alive from the lighter ammunition. It was decorated in dappled tan and brown, a testament to how much of his active service was spent in various sandboxes all over the world, with a fat tube slung under the barrel and a thick suppressor protruding over the end of it. He hefted it, picked up a twin magazine and seated it before pointing the barrel into a sand-filled steel tub and racking back the bolt to chamber a heavy round.

He filled his pouches with spare ammunition, enough to dangerously weigh down lesser men, before clipping the heavy rifle to the sling threaded under his vest. He selected two M9 Berettas, one going into a holster on his vest and the other into the drop-leg holster on his right thigh, and filled the similar rig on his left thigh with six spare magazines for the weapons. When he was finished, he looked less like a man and more like a one-man-band who played a multitude of different instruments. He cast his eye over the ranks of other weapons, the personal weapons of his team which they knew more intimately than they ever would their own families. He smiled a small smile, albeit one laced with sadness, that they were finally going to work.

Inside of a minute he was swiping himself into the accommodation block of the 160th Special Operations Aviation Regiment, or SOAR for short, and found them similarly climbing into their black flight suits.

His team had dedicated access to two MH-60L Black Hawk helicopters and their crew, as well as a support bird modified as a gunship with no troop-carrying capability. All three helicopters had extended fuel range, night vision enhanced sensors, and all were configured for stealth infiltration missions.

"Fully fueled and loaded, personal gear to a minimum, wheels up in twenty-five," he told them, nodding once before turning to leave again.

"Captain?" asked a female voice from down the corridor. Troy turned back to look at the speaker, Lieutenant Gina Pilloni, Sardinian by way of Birmingham, Alabama and the newest member of his extended team. She was young, too young in Troy's opinion to be worthy of a gig in SOAR, but she was confident, fit, and courageous. Being the lowest ranking, at least in experience, she was by far the baby of the group and was set apart as the only one not to have gone to war with them.

"Lieutenant?" Troy replied, not wanting a debate but unable to be openly hostile without provocation.

"Where are we going, sir?" she asked him, naivety and excitement showing evident on her face.

"To the helipad with minimal personal gear, fully fueled and loaded, in twenty-five," he answered patiently, then turned on his heel and left, leaving the six pilots and four crew to get it done.

Twenty-two minutes later, Troy stood on the tarmac in the dark as his team filed out and filtered into the two Black Hawks in their respective fire teams. They carried an array of personal weaponry as well as a large crate each between two of them. The odd man at the rear, and Troy's second-in-command, as well as fire team leader and long-time friend was Master Sergeant David White, better known as Chalky by the team. The military fashion for witty nicknames had long ceased to amaze either of them.

"I'm guessing this isn't my sudden call-up to OCS?" Chalky asked Troy as he approached, pushing another ammo crate on a trolley. Since completing his bachelor's degree by correspondence, Master Sergeant David White had formally been accepted to Officer Candidate School on an accelerated program for experienced NCOs.

"No," Troy told him, "this is for real."

Chalky shrugged, hefted the ammo crate onto the loading area of the helicopter, and turned to watch the trolley be blown across the tarmac by the rotor wash to fall on its side at the grass edge. Both Troy and Chalky watched in silence as the combined helicopter engines picked up their intensity to a screaming whine, then turned to their respective rides.

Two minutes later, a minute inside Troy's expected time of departure, each member of the combined twenty-person team designated Endeavor was aboard one of the three helicopters now hurtling low and fast over the camp. Each of them was wearing a headset which allowed comms with their team, and thanks to the encryption protocols, their team alone.

"Listen up," Troy told them though the boom mic attached to the headset he wore, "as of thirty minutes ago our beloved United States is at war." He paused to let that hang, knowing that his team were too professional to ask stupid questions in the middle of his brief. "We don't know who with as yet, but we do know that both eastern and western seaboards have been devastated by nuclear attacks. D.C. is gone and so is Fort Bragg, along with a half-dozen other cities. It's believed we were a target of an ICBM but it was intercepted by our ABMs." He paused, imagining the looks of horror and anger his team were exchanging, and even felt his own bird drop a little as though the pilot had been taken by the sudden shock of the news.

"Our orders are to get the fuck out of dodge and fall back on an enclosed position to await further orders from the remaining elements of command. Question time will be later, for now we wait for a deployment."

With that, he recited the coordinates of their target location from memory to the co-pilot and sat back.

A PERSON WITHOUT PRINCIPLES

Saturday 1:00 a.m. - Free America Movement Head-quarters

Colonel Glenn Butler had cleared all personnel from the command hut and sat at his desk in silence. The screens had been turned off as he couldn't bear to watch the unthinkable destruction being wrought on his country.

At first, he couldn't believe the coincidental timing of the attack happening just as the opening phase of his plan was drawing to a close. After the fourth mushroom cloud he saw on screen, the awareness slowly dawned on him that this was no mere coincidence, but a terrible country-wide campaign of annihilation and he had been responsible for effectively shutting down the command structure for whoever had used him like a pawn. All was lost, and worse than that; he was partially to blame. He had opened the door for them.

The phone chirped, making him jolt up in his seat in fright. There were noises outside as vehicles started and his so-called loyal followers fled, but the sudden sharpness and closeness of the ringer frightened him out of his stasis-like depression. He turned his attention to the CIA man on the other end of the line, preparing to launch into a savage and vitriolic rant about the irony of the word *intelligence* in their title.

"Butler," he snarled into the phone after raising the stubby aerial. He didn't wait for an answer but launched straight into is attack.

"Now you listen to me, you sorry piece of shit—" he started, but was cut off by laughing coming from the other end of the line.

"Colonel," said the voice in between chuckles, "I simply wanted to thank you for your kind assistance. You have been invaluable to the People's Republic."

With that the line went silent, and Colonel Glenn Butler slowly placed the phone on the table before him.

Sat back in a comfortable office chair on the other end of the line, the sound of a single sob escaping Butler's lips was quickly stifled. The ensuing silence, which hung heavy with an air of resolve, was punctuated only by the metallic sound of Butler's pistol protesting the action as he pulled back the top slide to chamber a round. A few seconds of heavy breathing followed before a single sharp report echoed down the line, then a noise that the man listening assumed to be a body slumping over. Waiting in silence with a partially amused look on his face, he heard the sounds of footsteps and a door opening. Shuffling noises merged into the sound of breathing as someone picked the phone up to their ear.

"It's done," said a female voice in a simple statement.

"Good," came the reply, "proceed as planned."

Suzanne clicked off the call and clipped the phone to her belt before looking down at the man sitting dead in his chair. The bear in the winter of life, the ageing lion superseded by a generation younger and fitter, the outcast silverback discarded and destined to die alone. She didn't even have pity for him any longer; she simply activated a fist-sized device which whirred quietly as it spun up and began to blink small LED lights. She tossed it onto Butler's dead lap and walked outside to climb into a truck and abandon the movement just as everyone else had.

Thirty-eight minutes after she had cleared the limits of the forest and headed north intending to head west on better roads, a single high-yield incendiary device dropped from near the stratosphere and plummeted earthwards like a dart, homing straight toward the signal emanating from the beacon, and wiped the Movement headquarters from the planet.

~

Further south, four people moved as fast as they could through the shadows of Central Park. The sound of sirens in the city was muted by their distance from the streets and shops which were being looted by everyone either too stupid, too selfish, or just totally unaware that nukes were dropping on the country. Trying to move around without attracting any attention to themselves was mostly simple, as the majority of people they saw had their own issues of more pressing concern than four strangers skulking west.

The majority, that was, with the exception of a young man having recently walked out of high school to walk a different path. His 'crew' made up entirely of children, only ever called him by his street name which, although apt, sounded comedic given his age. Muscle, a youth of fifteen but built like a man twice his age and heavy-set, watched them from the bushes and gave orders for two of his crew to follow them as he looped ahead.

This was a routine they had grown used to and, although they preferred to prey on naive tourists, it tended to work on New Yorkers who were supposed to be savvy enough not to get caught out like they did. Two hooded youths would follow the targets, staying close enough to unnerve them but never close enough to risk confrontation. When the nervous victims were spending more time looking behind them than in front, Muscle and the rest of the gang would burst from the bushes, beat their victims down, and rob them of everything.

The events in the city had led Muscle and his crew to step up their game that night, and already tonight they had committed dozens of felonies with impunity, as no cops ventured into the park that was their personal playground. They were encouraged into more bravery, more overt violence than normal, and now the reflected flash of metal he saw in the hands of one of them made him certain that he could now acquire the weapon he needed to be taken seriously on the streets. With a whistle and a nod of his head, two of the younger crew members, just thirteen and fourteen respectively, flicked up their hoods and set off into the darkness to set the trap.

~

Jake, at the head of their small advancing column, had his bright LED flashlight unclipped from his belt and held tactically in his left hand which he rested under his right as it gripped the Glock. He didn't have it turned on, as he would blind everyone and ruin the night vision all of their eyes had acquired. He would use it if he had to, but he knew the results all too well of losing his visual acuity in the dark because some idiot flashed a beam too close to his eyes. The brightness of it was a weapon in itself, both psychologically and for temporarily blinding suspects, and he intended to keep that in reserve, not least for the fact that everyone would be able to see them at a distance and not the other way around.

"Jake," said a voice softly from behind him, "we're being followed."

Jake froze and lowered his body weight instinctively on hearing the news. "Where?" he asked inadequately, when what he wanted to know were the answers to a dozen questions to correctly identify the threat and formulate the appropriate and accountable response.

"Two behind, hanging back," came Sebastian's voice, the smooth concierge showing an even more surprising skill-set with each minute that passed. "Keep moving slowly."

Jake resumed their cautious advance at the previous pace, his inherent obedience to receiving orders from senior ranks so ingrained that he didn't hesitate for a second. Not that he felt Sebastian was a senior rank, but something in the man's voice said he knew what he was doing, and moreover made Jake really believe it, so he did as he was told after making a mental note to ask why a hotel manager was seemingly trained in night operations.

"Keep moving," Sebastian said in the same low voice for the others to hear. "In a while they will probably block us in from the front and then try to rob us," he told them, hearing an alarmed noise from the traumatized Louise between Cal and Jake. Jake swallowed on hearing the words. He knew about the gang activity in Central Park to some degree, but being stationed miles—and in a tightly packed place like Manhattan a couple of miles was an eternity in terms of people and crime statistics—away from it down in the One-Three, he rarely needed the information. Plus, there was also a task force set up for that kind of thing when it rolled around as flavor of the month for the brass to throw overtime at.

Jake could imagine the CompStat meetings held at 1 Police Plaza, or 1PP as they liked to abbreviate it, where crime statistics were fed to a room full of brass and overtime budgets were thrown back casually as though money could prevent crime.

He changed his mind about his earlier decision not to give Louise a weapon, and took away the hand with the flashlight to unsnap the fastening of the compact 9mm under his left arm. Holding it out behind him to Louise he whispered, "Know how to use this?"

"Yes," she answered, taking the small gun and nestling it in her hand. A tense minute and a half later, Sebastian muttered two last instructions and then disappeared.

"Keep moving," he said, "and don't hit the flashlight until I call it." Then he was gone.

~

Muscle rolled his thick neck on his shoulders, put on his meanest game face, and stepped out to block the path. He could see them approaching, not clearly but more a sense of darker shadows moving amongst the dark shadows. Once more he saw the glint of reflection ahead, telling him that the gun was there and it would soon be his. Then he would be taken seriously. What he didn't see was any reflection from the black polymer of the three Glocks in the shadows ahead. Had he known, he would have hunted easier prey.

~

Just as a shadow ahead stepped out and partially sky lined itself on a slight incline, so too did the two followers pick up their pace to pen in the others. Sebastian, silently tucking himself into the foliage to his left and standing stock still with his breath held, felt the two pass right by him without ever knowing he was there. He slipped out and followed the unaware marauders on practiced feet, enjoying the adrenaline more than he thought he would. Sebastian Hill, remembering a life he tried so hard to escape and one he had promised, literally on pain of death, never to return to, suddenly found himself wondering why the hell he had ever retired. Hearing and sensing the inevitable confrontation ahead, he stalked forwards and struck twice, felling the two children with savage blows to their hoodie-covered skulls. Melting back into the undergrowth, he silently circled back around with a smile on his face which bordered on evil.

~

"Hand over everything," Muscle demanded confidently, flexing his upper body autonomously even though his intended victims wouldn't be able to see him sufficiently to fully appreciate the spectacle. A rustling to their right snatched their attention as two more figures emerged from the bushes, both brandishing reflective strips of sharp metal in their hands, held low but menacingly.

"Put your weapons down and step back," Jake told them in the unmistakable tone of voice of an eager cop. "Do it now and you can walk."

Muscle chuckled, a theatrical show of confidence which he actually felt, and sucked his teeth. He knew that people, especially cops, lived by rules. He felt free of rules and this empowered him, made him confident that he would easily triumph in this conflict even though he had literally brought a knife to a gunfight.

Jake drew in a breath to issue his next, and final, ultimatum when Sebastian struck. "Now!" he called, prompting Jake to hit the flashlight's switch with his thumb and cast a blinding light straight into the face of the one directly in his path.

Sebastian had worked around, smelled, and sensed the two others lurking in wait, and held his breath for them to spring their rudimentary trap. As he stepped forward and called out to Jake, he brought the butt of his weapon down onto the base of the skull of the man closest. The second one responded quicker than he expected, but he still had no chance.

He didn't realize this, because he was a young thug; full of the exuberance of angry youth and lawlessness, but with none of the calm confidence of experience and training. He was six feet from Sebastian, which was too far away to close the distance and stab him before he could fire, and too close to have any other options. His only chance of surviving the ambush was to surrender, but he failed to grasp that. The instant he made a move, Sebastian put two rounds dead center into his chest and killed him. He turned his attention to the one in front, who still had his hands up to shield his eyes from the bright light, and took three fast steps toward him. Sebastian kicked him brutally between the legs, which would have felled almost every person, man or woman, but it had the simple effect of doubling him over. Sebastian brought the gun down where his skull met his neck, but the exaggerated muscles of his upper back prevented the full effect from knocking him out. The second blow brought the huge youth to his knees, one hand on the tarmac of the path to steady himself.

"Come on!" Sebastian told them urgently, prompting the other three to follow. They ran, eager to put distance between themselves and the failed street robbery, with the bouncing beam of Jake's flashlight lighting their way. They didn't stop until they were forced to when Louise stumbled and fell in the dark, then they were forced to slow their pace.

~

Far behind them, having heard the shots and homing in on the sound like predators in the dark, two black-clad infiltrators found the three unconscious, one dead, and one injured youths on the park.

"Where did they go?" one asked the hugely muscled boy still gasping for breath.

"Go fuck yourself," he replied bravely, still believing that pure aggression and hostility were the only weapons at his disposal.

The man standing over him wasted no more time on questions, simply drew a bead on the likely path of his quarry and turned to put a single round into the heads of the entire crew at his feet.

RUN AND HIDE

Saturday 2:50 a.m. - Greenbrier Mountain, WV

Troy's unit touched down at the moth-balled forward operating base in the Allegheny Mountains in the dark; their expert pilots executed the maneuvers flawlessly using night vision. Troy had been there once with Chalky, travelling there in one of their dedicated Black Hawk helicopters and escorting a small flight of Chinooks, all weighted down with underslung loads. Whilst the Black Hawks could land easily on the artificially flattened earth, the Chinooks were too large to set down so had to hover whilst they took turns to cut away their cargo straps.

The location was not a new project. In fact, it harked back from even before the very beginnings of the Cold War, and was intended as a command bunker in the event of a nuclear attack. Whilst the enemy had changed drastically since then, the threat of nuclear annihilation had only ever grown in intensity, especially as Middle Eastern countries had since acquired their own nuclear arsenals. Not to mention the alarming amount of radioactive material which was unaccounted for since the fall of the iron curtain. The existence of a bunker in those mountains was not a state secret; in fact, the original cold war era bunker had been decommissioned and was now a novelty hotel, but the public never knew of the other base nestled into the dark hills.

Troy and a few other commanders of elite groups of specialists were read-in on certain contingency plans. They were all on code-word standby to drop everything they were doing and get their teams there with as much ammo as they could carry. Inside there was space for almost a hundred personnel. The base was buried deep into the very mountainside and had been excavated in parts over the last thirty years, as the emergency base was extended and refitted for various upgrades.

There were also vast stores held inside: MREs, munitions, telecoms suites, as well as huge fuel reservoirs and maintenance equipment to keep their birds in the air. The way the flattened helicopter pad had been created showed very little sign from any aerial surveillance and each helicopter could be covered with folding canopies. One by one the helicopters set down and shut down their engines as they disgorged their crew and passengers. Most of the operators, typical amongst their kind, had fallen back to sleep during the ride there but now came awake without any issues.

"Inside, grab a rack, find the briefing room in ten," Troy announced when the last sounds from the winding down engines had faded away. "Valdez, Farrell, get on overwatch. I'll fill you in later." The two teammates, inseparable at the best of times, nodded their assent.

Troy heard a muttered, "*Oohrah*" in stereo as the two trotted away to their assigned duty, which he translated into his own vernacular in his head. Commanding a team of mixed forces produced a lot of interesting cultural differences, and the *oohrah/hooah* debate between the army and the marines was a constant one which took a predictable turn when their resident SEAL piped up to offer his opinion on the matter.

Valdez, one of two trained and experienced snipers under his command, was a stone-cold killer who also had a passion for drawing landscapes in pencil; the pastime offering a stark contrast to his profession but also an insight into his love and deeply intrinsic knowledge of terrain. Farrell, his fellow United States Marine Corps recruit and friend, mocked his ability to find routes over open ground by telling others he had been a Coyote bringing illegals over the Mexican border. Valdez was from Houston, but that never stopped Farrell telling the story. He operated a big support weapon which he carried with ease, despite its incredible weight and his slight stature. Farrell operated as Valdez's eyes and protection detail, and between the two of them they had probably taken the lives of more insurgents in Iraq and Afghanistan than the decorated heroes Joe Public heard about. They didn't do what they did for fame, but because it was their job. Pure and simple.

Troy walked inside, leaving the aviators of SOAR running out the camouflage net canopies to cover their aircraft. Just as the operators of Endeavor cared for their weapons first, the 160th maintained their aircraft before themselves. He threw his ruck on the closest cot in the closest rack in the room nearest the ops center before pulling dust sheets off the table in the briefing room. As he did so under the weak glow of the emergency lighting, which had come on automatically when the main door had been opened, the main lighting came online. Troy smiled to himself knowing that Dillon, the team's proud tech geek, would have taken it upon himself to find the main power grid and fire it up. The bunker was powered by a generator as a backup, but one of the last changes to have been made was to reroute the entire power grid from a small hydro-electric plant submerged in the Greenbrier River. The facility, although officially decommissioned, was in fact a multi-billion-dollar project and one of the American military's best kept secrets.

A boot scuff behind him made him turn, and he found Chalky in the doorway of the windowless room. A puff of renewed air circulation dropped the temperature by a couple degrees as the airflow kicked up a gear to provide enough clean air for the bunker to support live bodies.

"So ..." Master Sergeant White said to him, waiting for the personal response to their mission before the official line was given to the team.

"Yeah," Troy said tiredly, adjusting his weapon, and sitting heavily, kicking up a small cloud of dust, "the shit has well and truly hit the fan, my friend."

"We're expecting more though, right?" Chalky asked him hopefully, meaning both in troops and information.

"Three of the standby teams on call to come here were at Bragg," Troy told him, meaning that they had lost close to a combined thousand years' worth of fighting experience in one go with the loss of the other teams like theirs along with their air support. "But we're supposed to be getting two Apaches from somewhere. ETA within the hour."

That was welcome news to Chalky's ears, after the crushing blow of discovering their 25 percent now had to act as the 100 percent they originally expected. There was almost nothing quite as lethal on the battlefield than a Boeing AH-64 Apache, and the chances of being supported by two of them to add to their strength would give them an incredible edge over any adversary.

"Well, shit ..." Chalky said before he puffed out his cheeks and blew out the air slowly. "I'll go find us some coffee." He walked out of the room, leaving Troy alone with his thoughts.

Five minutes later, having been hailed on the secure satphone from a pair of death-dealing air-sharks which hurtled toward their position hugging the terrain at close to 180 mph, he told his extended team to settle in until they arrived. He gulped down his second cup of coffee and took a lap of the main areas, finding the various members of his elite squad busying themselves with equipment or tech, and finding that their additional ammo cache had been carried to the closest armory. The screaming whine of four turboshaft engines penetrated the bunker, and he walked to the door to feel more than watch the angular aircraft settle down on the flat surface. Both aircraft were fully manned, with each pilot and co-pilot occupying their own sealed cockpit, and he watched through the thin moonlight as four men, *scratch that*, he thought, *three men and one woman*, based on how the hips of the first pilot swung, all walked toward him. He greeted them on the threshold, seeing that each of them only carried a small pack which would contain their emergency survival equipment. All of them wore M9 pistols similar to his own on their chests, and all of them had clearly abandoned sleep at a moment's notice when they got the call.

"You must be Gardner," said the man in the lead who had occupied the front seat of the second helicopter. "Colonel Simon, air force," he said introducing himself and offered a hand before turning to his other pilots. "Captains Rogers and Harley." Two men nodded to him, one bearing the call sign 'Buck' on his helmet. "Major Healey, army," he said, indicating at last the hip swinger. Troy shook hands with them in turn, noticing the Ranger patch on Healey's flight suit and trying not to raise his eyebrows. He was no misogynist, in fact he appreciated a fighting woman more than most, but finding, especially in this sudden shit storm, a young female army major who had success-fully attended ranger school was something of a rarity. It was commonplace for advanced-trained aircrew to train as infantry, given their close working relationships with the SF guys on the ground and their likelihood of being shot down in places less than hospitable. Also uncommon was the makeup of mixed arms helicopter crews. Troy assumed they were part of a cross-training exercise when they got the call.

"I'm Gardner, call me Troy," he told them. "Grab a coffee and meet in the briefing room when you're set. Empty bunks down the corridor to your left." They filed inside, loosening their tight flight suits and removing helmets as they passed him.

~

"Okay, so you're all clued up as much as I am with the exception of some bad news," Troy told the twenty-two people present; a few too many for the briefing room leaving a few guys standing. Not counting the two he had standing guard, this was his entire force, but as small as it was, it was certainly formidable. "Fort Bragg was hit by an ICBM, with an expected total loss. Three teams of SF which should have come here won't be coming at all." That news hung heavy in the room. The faces of his team registered the facts with anger, processed it, and set it aside to use later. It was clear from the reactions of the Apache crews that they already knew this, but some of the pilots and crew of the 160th cracked at the news.

"We are waiting for orders and intelligence for counter-strikes, but until such time as we are deployed our mission is to sit tight and wait." He held up both hands to stay the barrage of protests he knew would come. "I know, I hate that shit just as much as everyone here, but it's what we're going to do. Any questions?" By telling them that they now had to sit on their asses and wait to be set on something to kill, he expected few questions.

"Command element and reinforcements?" Dillon asked from a seat near the front.

"Unknown on any other personnel," Troy said, "and command elements are still in play from unknown locations. Comms via satphone and squad net, which I need you to re-encrypt and rotate. Assume we are compromised by any other means of communication, got it?" They did, so Troy dismissed them, knowing that they would do whatever tasks were necessary without orders.

"Jackson, Miller," Chalky called out making two men stop and turn, "relieve Valdez and Farrell. Send them to me for the brief." The two men acknowledged their orders and left.

"Go do your rounds," Chalky told Troy. "I'll fill in the others."

Troy nodded to his friend and set down his coffee cup.

THE GREATEST VICTORY

Saturday 6 p.m. Local Time, Beijing

"His Excellency will see you now," the aide told her, prompting her to stand and smooth down the plain black suit she had been wearing for an entire night and a day. Various high-ranking officials also stood, resplendent in their crisply pressed dress uniforms in honor of seeing the President of the People's Republic of China face-to-face.

They entered the grand office to find the man himself stood looking out of the huge glass wall over the city sprawling below. Two aides busied themselves in the room and now gathered papers before bowing and leaving, shutting the double doors as they went. All of the invited guests bowed low, waiting for their leader to acknowledge them. He turned, bowed in response, and sat at his desk.

"Tell me," he began, "how is the operation developing?"

A man stepped forward quickly, bowing again, and gave the report from the perspective of the bombing runs to list a series of grand successes, with his eagerness for praise making the woman in the black suit mindful of a puppy. The president nodded his understanding, then asked for a report on the ballistic missile strikes. His brow wrinkled once on hearing that a missile destined for one of the largest US military bases had been intercepted by advanced anti-ballistic missile technology which they neither knew about or possessed an equal.

"And we are certain that the origin of the attack is not known?" he asked, interrupting the puppy. Silence in the room allowed her to clear her throat and take half a step forward to sketch a further small bow.

"Nothing indicates that they are aware it was us," she said, her voice sounding cool and confident in contrast to the excited and nervous generals now standing slightly behind her. "And the majority of primary and secondary targets are on course to be destroyed by tonight. We are ready for the next phase, Your Excellency," she said, bowing again but not stepping backwards.

The president thought for a few seconds before glancing up and locking eyes with her.

"Proceed," he told her, and seemed to tell her alone, before waving a hand and dismissing them all. They bowed and left the office.

"One moment," he called after them, making all of them turn, hopeful that they had been addressed personally, but they saw that he was only looking at the woman in the creased black suit. She walked back inside leaving the gaggle of disappointed uniforms behind and flashed them a small smile as she closed the doors herself.

"Your Excellency?" she enquired politely as she approached.

"I am surprised to see you here," he told her, still not looking at her but keeping his eyes on the papers on his desk. "I was expecting your superior."

"He is resting, Excellency. It has been a long night," she said carefully.

"And a longer day," replied the president, looking up at her as he leaned back in his chair, "but I suspect you haven't stopped to rest."

"No, Excellency," she answered with a depreciating smile. "I have not."

"I like that," he told her, "it shows dedication and commitment. Now, take this"—he handed her something the size of a business card—"and report to me directly whenever you need to."

She took the card and bowed. Turning back from the door she took a gamble and glanced back.

"Thank you, Uncle," she said, risking his displeasure by reminding him of their family connection. He smiled a small admonishment at his niece, and waved her away with a final piece of advice.

"The greatest victory is that which requires no battle," he told her, his meaning obvious; he wanted little or no casualties in the next phase of the operation.

She walked away, the quote bouncing around in her brain as she tried to fathom how the remaining population of the United States could be subdued without casualties. Still, already on their way to the continent was a land force the size of which had not been seen since the combined western nations invaded Iraq, and she doubted that any shattered remnants of the American military could withstand that without air superiority and an intact command structure. After grabbing ten minutes sleep in the car on the way back to the command center, she pulled a bag from the trunk and strode inside, bypassing the security station without question.

Now, dressed in a fresh black suit and white blouse, she gave the order to invade, not waiting for confirmation from her superiors.

SHOWS HOW MUCH YOU KNOW A PERSON

Saturday 5 a.m. - 79th Street Basin, NYC

After their flight from the dangers of Central Park during a blackout and in the midst of anarchy, the four unlikely allies helped themselves to transport at a CitiBike stand by 72nd Street. All four were quiet, mostly for their own reasons, and none of them had much in the way of breath to spare. Blasting through the streets, weaving around abandoned cars and dodging looters, they had a tense moment as they had to divert the inferno that had once been a massive department store. Eventually hitting Riverside Drive, they turned north again, abandoning the bikes at the 79th Street Basin.

It seemed that they weren't the only ones with the same idea, and the rows of empty moorings were testament to that. Sebastian peered through the light of the pre-dawn to find his own boat, breathing out a sigh of relief that it was still there. The basin operated a boat office by the café, and the others followed Sebastian's obvious lead as he strode toward it, kicking in the wooden door without even checking if it was open. He hit the lock of a metal cabinet twice with the butt of his gun, opened it and ran his fingers over the ranks of keys until he found the right mooring number. Grabbing the keys on the big, floating keychain he turned and went back outside.

Leading the way along the wooden pier, he stopped at a small fishing vessel with a covered pilot deck and froze.

The characteristic sound of a shotgun being pumped to chamber a round chilled their spines in unison. Sebastian slowly holstered his gun and held his hands aloft as he turned.

"It's okay, Jake," he said, trying to reassure the young cop that he didn't need to try and take charge. "Cal, Louise, lower your weapons."

As suddenly as he had frozen, he now dropped his hands and laughed.

"Jesus, brother, you scared the shit out of me!" he said, stepping forward and grabbing the man with shotgun in a tight embrace. The two men rocked back and forth as they hugged it out, laughing.

"I've been here since midnight," the man with the shotgun said, disengaging. "I was starting to think you wouldn't make it."

"Me? Come on, man ..." Sebastian said, hands out wide and wearing a smile. "Nothing's killed me yet!"

"Cal, Jake, Louise, this is my friend," he said. "Meet Joe Wilkins. CIA"

Joe hit him in the shoulder. "Asshole, you're not supposed to tell people that," he said.

"That explains a lot," Jake said, shaking the man's hand. "I'm guessing that's where you learned to do all that stuff?" he said to Sebastian.

"Yeah," he replied, "retired two years ago."

"Well, not really retired …" Joe said, smiling more broadly.

"Enough about that," Sebastian said quickly, changing the subject. "Any calls?" he asked his former colleague.

"Nothing," he said seriously, "protocols to head north are in play." Sebastian turned to the others.

"We're heading for Canada to reform. You're welcome to join us," he told them.

The three of them looked at each other.

"I'm going home, to West Virginia" Louise said groggily. Cal tried to be gallant and said that he was staying with her to make sure she got back safely. Jake was torn between rejoining the fight against terror and protecting civilians, but just behind the first thought came the realization that any government base would likely be a target and heading inland to get off the grid was a safer option. He wanted to say that he would head home, find his family, but he knew that the likelihood of finding them safe as he headed toward a nuclear fallout cloud was less than sensible.

"Okay," Sebastian said, "we'll take you to the other side of the Hudson." He unclipped the duty belt and handed it back to Jake as he stepped down to the deck. Jake began to respond as Sebastian used the keys to open the heavy tackle box built into the boat's furniture. Before the cop could offer for him to keep the weapon, he straightened with a compact submachine gun and slapped in a magazine before tossing it to Joe. Jake kept quiet about his offer to give up a single Glock.

They cast off inside of two minutes, Sebastian revving the boat's engine and pointing them west. Jake stole a look into the box to see more weaponry on show before he summed up the courage to ask if he could play with another boy's toys.

~

Two men dressed in black and carrying suppressed assault weapons jogged onto the pier just as the five people floated away from the wooden walkway. The leader stopped and pulled a face, knowing that his quarry had escaped, even if it was only a personal mission and not critical to the overall plan. His backup raised his weapon and leaned into it, taking a bead on the back of the vessel. A hand appeared on the rifle stock and gently lowered it before he was spoken to in Mandarin.

"Leave them," he said, "signal the rest of the team to pull back."

~

"Any chance of the Mossberg?" Jake asked, indicating the shotgun that Joe had brought with him. Joe and Sebastian exchanged a look, the latter nodding to his friend, and Jake was happily reunited with some heavier weaponry. Cal was now wearing the duty belt and the chrome semi-auto had made its way into the bag he carried.

It took them twenty minutes with the cold, watery air stinging their faces to cross. Sebastian throttled down and turned the boat to allow it to bump against a wooden pier where Joe threw a lashing line over a post to hold them steady. The three of them climbed unsteadily to dry land and turned to face the others.

"My advice," Sebastian said seriously, "is to get a car and head west, but stay off the main road and away from big towns unless absolutely necessary. Good luck," he said, turning away to power the boat back out into open water.

The three stood on the side of the river and watched the boat motor away, all of them wondering if they had made the right choice. To Cal, his two companions were invaluable. He was a stranger in the country, totally unaware of the customs and cultures and still not possessing even the slightest clue about how big the continent truly was.

"There's a dealership just north of here," Jake said, "come on." He set off, not waiting for the others to follow. Louise was still quiet, almost catatonic and didn't answer either of them when they spoke. Cal took her left hand after switching the Glock to his left and half pulled her along. Finding the dealership in an alarmingly empty street devoid of activity, Jake told them to wait while he looked around. Cal tried to figure out why nobody was fleeing in panic, but guessed that most had either already left or were simply asleep as normal, like the events on Manhattan didn't affect them.

"It's locked up," Jake said as he returned to them. "We'll need to break in." Cal nodded his agreement, leading Louise after him and growing more concerned that she may be in shock.

"Jake," he said, "she's exhausted or in shock or something, she needs to rest." Jake looked at her, seeing a vacancy in her eyes and pursing his lips as he thought.

"Car first, rest after," he said.

He led them on a short lap of the forecourt, knowing that they would never get one of the premium vehicles from inside through the huge glass walls. Pointing out a pickup truck to Cal and gaining agreement, they went back to the entrance. Breaking a panel in the glass door Jake leaned in and flipped the bolts, pushing the door open over the protesting screams of glass catching on metal. Walking confidently into the sales office he repeated the actions of Sebastian on the other side of the river and forced open the key locker. He found a selection of Ford keys and took them outside to press the buttons in turn, until one was rewarded with a flash as the doors unlocked.

They piled into the truck, throwing the big price tag from the window onto the ground. Jake backed it out carefully and slid the selector into drive. Driving through the mostly empty streets and out into more open country, Cal saw the young cop nodding his head and struggling to maintain a steady 60 mph.

"Okay," he said, "we need to stop." Jake was too exhausted to offer any disagreement. The adrenaline-fueled night on the run and the gunfights had taken almost everything from him both physically and emotionally. He pulled the truck off the road, killed the engine, and fell back in his seat. Cal did the same, after looking behind to see Louise fast asleep on the back seat. Closing his eyes, exhaustion soon took him too.

Saturday 10 a.m. - Outside Newark, New Jersey

Cal woke with a start, dragged from sleep by something he couldn't yet figure out. Looking over at Jake, he saw that their driver was still asleep and slumped against the window. He realized that the sound which had alerted him to something being wrong, which had dragged him from unconsciousness, was the panicked clicking of the rear door handle and rapid breathing with it.

Spinning in his seat, he startled Louise who was trying desperately to open the door but uncomprehending that they were locked, and Jake was sat in front of the controls to release them. On seeing Cal, Louise snatched up the compact pistol next to her, Jake's backup weapon which he had never taken back from her, and pointed at his face.

He threw both hands up in a movement so rapid that he woke Jake with a start and prompted him to swing his head left and right looking for a threat outside the steamed-up glass of the cab, only to realize that Cal's eyes were fixed on the back seat. Spinning to look, he froze as the terrified face of Louise stared at them over the top of his own gun as she switched her aim in turn. Both men started to speak at once.

"Louise, it's okay—" said Cal.

"What the hell?" was Jake's response.

Louise said nothing. Her mouth moved as though she wanted to speak but hadn't done so in so long that the ability to converse was evading her. Her brow furrowed in what looked like severe confusion. The little finger of her right hand, clamped so tightly around the stubby pistol grip that her knuckles showed white, twitched involuntarily. She glanced around, looking out of the windows to try and make sense of what she saw. She still couldn't speak and looked more and more like her panic and frustration would cause her to squeeze one pound of pressure too much on the trigger of the compact Glock in her hand. Her skin was pale but appeared wet with a sheen of sweat over her face, and the shakes competed with the twitching of her fingers to totally transform the woman they had fled with—that Cal had spent two days with—into someone they didn't recognize. Nor, did it seem, that she recognized them.

Slowly, Jake opened his door and activated the central locking to produce a click from all four doors. Louise didn't register this other than to look at the source of the noise, which made no logical sense if she wanted to escape the confines of the truck. Jake slipped his legs and body from the open door, never taking his eyes off her, but she didn't react to him. Cal glanced at Jake, then did the same out of the passenger side. Louise stayed staring forwards, not responding. Both men stepped carefully away from the truck, neither of them understanding the sudden change in her behavior. She had been distant ever since the hotel, but then she had shot and killed someone about to kill Cal. She had been quiet throughout their adrenaline-fueled flight from New York, and was almost catatonic when they had reached the far side of the Hudson River, but now they were faced with what seemed like a completely different person. Jake snapped his fingers for Cal's attention, then motioned for him to go to the rear side door which was furthest away from her. He stepped carefully toward the side she was sat on, and spoke to Cal.

"Open it, carefully," he told him.

He did, and Louise's eyes turned slowly toward him as she still held the gun tightly pointed forwards at the windshield.

Jake stepped close, snatched the door open and clamped a hand hard over the top of the gun, trying to block the topslide from working even if she pulled the trigger. He pulled the gun easily from her grasp as she turned her head toward him and recoiled, letting the gun be taken from her hands. She still seemed utterly bewildered about what was going on.

"Louise!" Cal said, making her slowly turn her head back toward him and stare with seemingly unseeing eyes. "What's wrong?"

She didn't answer, just stared at him blankly wearing a confused look of anger.

"She doesn't look so good," Jake said. "Has she got any medical conditions?"

Cal had to admit that he didn't know. Hell, he barely knew the girl having only just met her.

"Louise," Jake said as he checked the chamber of the Glock and worryingly found it charged with a reflective piece of brass before holstering it back under his arm, "can you understand me?" he said slowly as though talking to an infant or a non-English speaker. She stared at him without responding. The two men looked at each other and Jake shrugged.

"Could be something medical," he said, "could be shock ..."

"It's like she's sleepwalking," Cal said, seeing an instant reaction to his words on Jake's face.

"Wait here with her," he said, turning on his heel and jogging toward the rest stop. He stopped at a vending machine and dug in his pocket for change, then stopped and—for the first time in his life—knowingly committed a crime. He put his heavy boot straight through the glass front, and used the barrel of his pistol to knock away the shards sticking out at sharp angles. He grabbed a handful of candy bars. Jogging back to the truck he spilled the contents of his arms onto the driver's seat, unwrapped a candy bar and handed it tentatively to the girl.

"Eat something," Jake said, "please?"

Almost zombie-like in her twitching movements she took the bar, but glanced back and forth between Cal and Jake as though she still tried to understand what had happened. She ate, small bites and slow chewing, taking tense minutes to finish it. Jake unwrapped another and handed it to her, this one going down in half the time.

"Where are we?" she asked in a small voice, finally.

Cal and Jake glanced at each other, the relief evident on both of their faces that she seemed to be coming out of whatever state she had lapsed into.

"Newark," Jake said. Cal realized he didn't know where Newark was.

"My bag," Louise said quietly, looking left and right forlornly.

"You left it at the hotel, we had to run," Cal told her.

"I need my bag," she said again, "my insulin kit."

Both men sagged with sudden understanding. In their flight from Manhattan in a wash of adrenaline, of the gunfights and the fear of bombs and mushroom clouds, they had run with the clothes on their backs. Realizing now that her blood sugar must have dropped dangerously low, but was masked by the adrenaline, and had fallen far beyond even low levels for normal behavior when she slept, Louise had fallen into a hypoglycemic state and woken up without the first clue where she was and what had happened.

As her faculties slowly returned, the sugar in the food being absorbed into her bloodstream, they filled her in on the events of the last few hours. She listened in silence, glancing between the two of them as they picked up the story from their own perspectives, until the events caught up to where they were now: tucked away from the main streets of Newark having caught a short sleep.

"We'll find a pharmacy or something," Cal reassured her, "first priority."

But the first priority was now escaping. Muted crumping noises battled against the barely perceptible changes in air pressure, but the flashes of light on the eastern horizon was unmistakable. Cal instinctively looked up, sensing more than thinking that the explosions were falling from the sky rather than detonating at ground level, but he could see or hear no planes. As New York city on the far side of the distant river was ravaged first, the bombs then fell on the western side of the Hudson, and began dropping closer to them.

"Time to go," Jake said, throwing himself behind the wheel and gunning the engine, "and let's just hope there's no more nukes coming."

THE SYSTEMATIC APPROACH

Saturday 10:30 p.m. Local Time, Beijing

The dark-suited woman had taken a small break, swiping a keycard into the unmarked suite of secure offices in the building one floor up from the command center. She had showered, put on the same dark suit and pale blue blouse this time. Now that she smelled and felt clean, she took two more of the stimulant tablets she had been surviving on for two days and washed them down with water.

Walking out of the frosted glass doors she refused to wait for the elevator for a single floor and took the stairs. Whether it was quicker or not was irrelevant; she was not the kind of woman who could stand still. She strode straight back into the secure command center, bypassing the security station entirely as though they weren't even there, and walked unchallenged onto the floor. She glanced around, saw that the old man had taken himself away, and asked for a report on what she had missed. The supervisor looked nervous, mostly because he had little to report seeing as she'd only been gone for about forty minutes.

"Bombing is underway," he told her, trying to stick to the bare facts in case he annoyed her. "We are getting reports of successes for military camps, airfields, naval bases, infrastructure, emergency response ..." He trailed away, not sure what else she wanted to hear.

She said nothing but lit another cigarette without taking her eyes off him.

"Good," she said finally, putting the lighter back into a jacket pocket, "when will the second wave be ready?"

He swallowed, checking the information on his tablet even though he knew the answer. "Bombers are returning now, they should be refitted and refueled and back in the air in less than three hours."

She turned to regard him coldly. She knew as well as he did that the inescapable laws of physics were just that: inescapable. Both of them knew that there was no way to get more planes in the air any faster, nor could anyone issue an order for an ICBM launch as the Americans had already proven their anti-ballistic weapons shield was more than operational. Their prototype nuclear submarine was sailing south in the Atlantic to take on more missiles, then it would be back to prowl the eastern seaboard. It was there primarily to prevent any other countries coming to the aid of the Americans, and their backup was already steaming toward them to complete the underwater shield.

Their carrier group, on the other side of the continent, was steaming eastwards to close the distance and increase their 'play' time. The net was pulling tight, the rest of the world still had no idea that they were responsible, and within twelve hours they would have boots on the ground other than their insurgency teams.

Every target which could offer them resistance, every military base which could slow the advance of their invasion, was being systematically destroyed state by state, and the population was being driven from the big cities on the coast where the survivors could be corralled, catalogued, and put to work.

The ministry had done their shady work, and had successfully puppeted the rogue Americans into taking out the leadership with the ability to counter-launch nuclear missiles, and with the president and the vice president both in the White House when it was obliterated by nuclear fire, their enemy had nobody available with the authority to order any such strike, even if they knew who to launch against.

Saturday 10:40 a.m. - Highway 64, Outside Charlestown

Speaker of the house, Madeline Tanner, sat in the back of the lead Chevy Tahoe as it sped east. Her secret service detail of five men and one woman drove fast, nose to tail, with their lights flashing. Weaving through the sparse traffic like an angry black snake, the radio in the front seat barked to life and prompted them to slow.

"What's going on?" Madeline asked as she leaned her head through. She wasn't used to riding in the lead car, as they normally held her securely in the middle car with protection front and rear. The head of her team, Drew Briar, a former US Marine with more than enough experience of vehicle convoy ambushes, liked to mix it up and keep any potential threat guessing as to which car she was in. Leaning back to shout over the road noise, he answered her whilst keeping his eyes on the road. "We need to get off the highway, ma'am," he told her, "got reports of aerial bombardments and need you away from population centers."

Madeline sat back, wishing now that she had read the Secret Service protocols for keeping their principles safe.

"We paint by numbers," he called behind his shoulder again, "we need to get you secured and see what we're dealing with."

Madeline nodded, not realizing she had forgotten to answer him out loud. She had been born into a life of politics, although she had never once regretted it. Working on her father's campaign for Governorship of their home state even before she had started school, she had loved the life and had always shown a talent for it. Her rise to the Senate via state Governor was, for her and everyone who knew her, an inevitability.

A short term as majority whip led to a fortuitous placement when the last speaker retired, and Madeline found herself appointed by the house. The president and the VP had both come up the political ranks with her, had both served in the Senate with her, and she considered both to be something nearing friends. Learning that both were now dead, and that the Capitol was annihilated by a nuclear strike, had turned her world upside down.

It was fortuitous timing again that had saved her from sharing their fate, as she had left her office at a dead run not forty-eight hours before when her sister had called to say that their mom had suffered a stroke. Drew, implacable as ever, had called for three cars to be ready and taken two thirds of her entire detail. There was little chance of calling up a chopper for the journey, instead he had led the convoy as he did now only with sirens blaring and local law enforcement standing by to escort them. In the end, she had been too late to see her mother before she passed, but she stayed to console her sister who had been with her until the very end. She was glad that her mom had passed, for the simple reason that she would never know their beloved country now lay a third in ruins, with worse yet to come.

So now she sat back, shot a glance at her terrified head of staff who had insisted on accompanying her, and trusted her security detail to do what they did best. They were getting her off the highway, and after that god only knew what would happen.

Saturday 10:59 a.m. - Greenbrier Mountain, WV

"Gardner, Dillon," came the low voice in Troy's earpiece. He had taken his turn on stag relieving Miller and Jackson—two Marines with as dizzying a skillset as the rest of his team—and was sat still in line of sight with their quietest member. Although usually paired on missions with Chalky, he would not let both of their nominal commanders be away from the command center at the same time.

"Yeah," he said into his mic, "what's up?" Radio discipline was for the grunts.

"Incoming message via secure satellite server," Dillon told him. "I'll need to decrypt it first."

Troy, his interest more than piqued, cast a look over to Ghost. He had heard the same transmission, everyone on their secure squad net had heard it, so Ghost simply nodded to say that he was good until someone else came to take over Troy's duties. Ghost's real name was Clay, and he had left law enforcement and the LAPD SWAT team behind to join the 101st Airborne, but much else about the man was a mystery. He could glide in and out of rooms without people knowing he was there, which had quickly earned him the nickname. Normally Troy would need to know a lot more about a man before he stayed on the team, as personalities clashed horribly sometimes, but Ghost was not a man to upset people, and his insane infiltration skills and ability to defeat locks was a major pull. He had stayed, and he was happy being the silent partner in the team. That wasn't to say that quiet was his default setting in combat, and his uncanny skill at skydiving was testimony to his bravery.

"Bones, Gardner," he said into his mic again as he stood and made for the bunker entrance.

"On my way," came the response, needing no answer. It left a feeling of satisfaction in Troy's chest that his team were just as switched-on as ever, despite the shit storm they were all now in.

Bones, real name Andy Bonham, was the team's only SEAL; a fact which he was never allowed to forget. The majority were marines, albeit from different specialisms to give their team the vast array of skills needed as a collective, and both Troy and Chalky were Rangers through and through, but their resident SEAL was alone in his discipline. As the team medic, medic being a technical term as he was so highly qualified and experienced that in just about every country in the world he would be called a doctor, he had been introduced as their new sawbones, and the nickname had stuck from day one. Whether he had a nickname already was a fact not featuring on the relevance scale, but he had demonstrated his ability not only to diagnose and undertake emergency field surgery to save the life of a marine injured by an explosion on their last tour, but he had done so under sparse cover and whilst being the subject of a half-dozen interested Taliban, each showering him with gifts of incoming

7.62. He had completed the surgery in record time—record time for a surgeon in a hospital—closed off the bleeding arteries and stitched the guy back up. He then pulled the guy's camera from the pouch on his webbing, snapped them a blood-soaked selfie as the injured man raised a shaky thumb and cracked a grin through the pain, then went on to assist in eliminating the enemy threat. Troy suspected that the man's heart beat maybe two or three times a minute, because he never once seemed under pressure.

The two men passed in the entrance, exchanging a nod as they squeezed in to make the necessary space for two big men in full war gear, and Troy carried on to the command center where Dillon was showing a woman with dark hair how to reprogram their radios. Dropping his multitasking with Gina, the young pilot who always seemed to be pissed at Troy, he tore off the sheet of paper which had been decrypted and was just finishing rolling off the old-fashioned printer. Without reading it first, he handed it to Troy who calibrated the appropriate arm length to read the small print; he still refused to admit that reading glasses were an enemy looming over the near horizon. Troy read in silence before lowering the paper and hitting his radio transmit button.

"Everyone to the briefing room," he called simply. Knowing that the sentries posted outside would assume that this didn't include them, he added, "Bones and Ghost too." He glanced at Gina. "Round up the rest of the *Night Stalkers*," he instructed, prompting a smile of pride at his use of her unit's special moniker. He looked to Dillon, "Get the Apache crews?" Dillon nodded, and Troy was left alone looking at the report again.

"Command elements are still active in Alaska," Troy told the assembled and extended team, all crammed into the small room. "Anti-Ballistic Missile site is still active but bombing and nukes have crippled the military and law enforcement. We have no carriers stateside, and just about every base has been hit." He paused, not relishing giving the information he was about to repeat. "That includes Fort Campbell. Anyone still on base as of 0900 is gone." He let that hang, hoping that they all got the subtext that they were likely the only intact unit to escape the base.

He scanned for reactions in the room. His operators all wore stony expressions; no weakness broke through their exteriors but the pilots all reacted. They weren't top tier operators, but they were experienced and disciplined enough not to shout out pointless questions.

"And now for the bad news," Troy said, earning a few raised eyebrows from his team. "D.C. is gone so we currently have no Commander in Chief. Also," he said, telling them that shit did indeed get worse, "Alaska is tracking a serious amount of incoming. Likely an invasion force." That did spark a question, and it came from Air Force Colonel Simon. Troy looked at the man, seeing his slightly pale but intense face wearing a mask of thinly veiled murder. "NorKs?" he asked.

"Unknown at this time," Troy said, suspecting that the North Koreans would have an interest in any attack on the US, "but attacks have also come from the east coast so we don't know who our enemy is yet, and we have to be prepared that it's not just one enemy"—he cut the speculation off there—"that may or may not be something which hits our radar soon, but first we have a mission," he told them, seeing trepidation overtaken by eagerness on more than the nine faces he expected it from.

HEADING OUT WEST

Saturday, 12:18 p.m. - Highway 78, Near Clinton

The three occupants of the truck were exhausted but tried not to let it affect them. They switched drivers often as none of them had slept for almost two days and even then, the excitement had prevented that sleep from being a full recharge. Now they were fleeing, heading inland as fast as they could.

After the initial attacks and the chaos which had spread across Manhattan, things had started to happen which weren't in their game plan. Leland Puller, in breach of all protocol, had used the burner cell to call the number which had given him the command to begin, but as he expected it was dead. He destroyed the SIM card and broke the phone in half, allowing some of his frustrations to pour out in the small act of destruction. After it was clear that the bombs and fires weren't anything to do with any plan they had been read in on, they still stayed put believing that it was an OpSec issue; there were other Movement soldiers in play in the city that they didn't know about. That notion was abandoned as soon as the news reports showed nuclear attacks on both east and west coasts.

Committed to the cause or not, that shit he just wasn't down with.

He decided it was time to leave, leave everything, but they were trapped in the maelstrom they had helped create. Two of the Movement soldiers stuck to him like glue, both former marines and inexorably drawn back to the command of something—someone—they felt comfortable following. Leland hefted his AR15, strapped in, and set off into the streets with his two marines trying to match his pace. The sight of three armed men skulking along in the shadows raised sufficient suspicion to earn a challenge from a pair of NYPD cops, and the ensuing gun fight was brief but bloody. The heavier caliber of their weapons, combined with the far superior rate of fire and the sheer element of surprise when they opened up left the two cops dead, and they ran before they attracted more attention that required a ballistic response.

Even though the echoes of peak physical fitness still sounded quietly in their heads, neither had maintained themselves to a standard to match Leland's and he found himself facing the choice to rest them or leave them behind. Kicking in the side door of a small store he rested them for a few hours before they became liabilities. In the pre-dawn he woke them, setting a slower pace on the short distance to the river to find a way across.

It may not have been the decent thing to do, but forcing their way onto an already overloaded NYPD patrol boat and making most of the passenger get off to stay in the chaos of the city was the only way they could guarantee their escape. The uniformed man they disarmed and held at gunpoint whilst he drove them to the far side of the Hudson River cried the entire time it took to cross, and he clearly expected them to kill him as his look of shock was almost funny when they simply walked away. The man turned his boat and gunned it toward Manhattan, hoping that his family and friends were still waiting for him.

As Leland and his two ageing former marines walked away from the pier they all ducked instinctively as the first bombs fell in the very spot they had, until recently, occupied. They exchanged looks of horrified misunderstanding.

"Definitely not us," Leland said turning away and stepping out into the street directly in the path of an oncoming truck. He raised his rifle and seeing no response from the driver, put a single round into the windshield three feet to the guys right side. The truck slowed and stopped, the door of the cab opened, and a man got out to fall over at the side of the road. Scrambling to his feet, he ran.

"This is us," he said, lowering his rifle but keeping it in the low ready position. Climbing inside the big cab and squeezing the three of them along the bench seat, they set their collective sights west and stopped for nothing.

Now, miles clear of the heavily populated areas and thinking themselves lucky that they weren't caught in the bombing, they were suffering the onset of exhaustion and had to stop.

"What's the plan then, Gunny?" the passenger on the right asked Leland. He knew little about either of them, but had heard him called Cobb by the other. He looked across at them after killing the engine and rubbed his eyes.

"I'm heading to Pittsburgh," he told them. "I've got people there."

"And after that?" asked the one who wasn't Cobb.

"After that, I'm heading for the Kentucky militia," he told them.

Cobb and Not Cobb looked at each other and then back to Leland.

"Why Kentucky?" Not Cobb asked.

"Boys," Leland said wistfully, "an Alabama tick ain't got nothing on them Kentucky boys when they're holed up in their *hollers*."

Seeing as Cobb and Not Cobb didn't have a better suggestion, both of them were happy to tag along.

Saturday, 1:12 p.m. - Still Valley, NJ

"There," Cal said, pointing to a sign, "pharmacy." He glanced behind to see Louise opening and closing her mouth absently. She had drunk all of the drinks they had with them, but still complained of feeling thirsty. Cal had no doubt she could manage herself effectively with medication, but without it and having spent a night and a day on the run she was slipping in and out of cohesion. She wavered between twitchy and anxious, to sluggish and absent. Jake said nothing, but pulled off the main street in response.

Pulling up directly outside the large store, Cal saw that it was the kind of place which sold everything from tools to groceries, and had probably been family-owned for at least a couple of generations before the franchise owning the pharmacy spread out like fungus and swallowed up the small business.

The two men got out of the cab and drew their guns; Cal the Glock and Jake pulling the butt of the Mossberg into his shoulder and tugging it close with the barrel depressed to the ground. The place seemed deserted, although the sounds of cars on the highway nearby were loud with horns blasting as what seemed like the whole of Jersey headed west. There were signs that people had come by, but the place didn't seem to have been ransacked from the outside. Finding the door open, Jake glanced to Cal to check if he was ready, and shouldered it open slowly to enter at a crouch with his eyes always pointing in the same direction as the barrel of the shotgun. A gentle tinkle of a bell above the door made the cop curse himself for not seeing it in time to prevent their entrance being announced. In spite of Jake's training, they were instantly blindsided and the sound of another shotgun pumping a shell into the chamber was unmistakable.

"That's far enough," said an accented voice from behind a low counter, "drop your weapons, please."

The manners are an interesting touch, though Cal, *especially when being held at gunpoint.* Jake took over the negotiations, speaking as he often did like he was reciting the NYPD playbook.

"Okay, sir," he said, taking his left hand away from the stock of his gun to appear less hostile but keeping his right hand by the trigger grip. "We don't mean any harm and we don't want any trouble; we've got a young lady in our care who needs medical attention."

As they both turned slowly, Cal's eyes rested on a short man with smooth, rich brown skin and a jet-black beard. He wore a plain white shirt, collarless and done up to the very top, and a flash of brilliantly white teeth shone out between mustache and beard, and bright eyes shone out between mustache and the bright turban on his head. He held the gun uncertainly, like he wasn't used to handling firearms, and Cal was sure that if he pulled the trigger the way he was holding the stock then the recoil would likely slam it into his face and remove those white teeth.

"What kind of medical attention?" he asked, not changing the aim of the shotgun.

"She's diabetic, and she needs insulin," Cal said. He opened his mouth to say more but the man cut him off.

"When did she last inject, and what is her blood sugar like?" he asked intensely, his accent clearly not Americanized but easily understandable.

"Yesterday, and she crashed out in the night, woke up all confused so we gave her candy and she got better for a while," Jake told him.

The man lowered his gun slightly, as if fighting an internal battle between self-preservation and helping others. "Bring her inside," he told them, lowering the gun and placing it on the counter like his hands had been dirtied by it. "And be quick," he added.

Both Cal and Jake did as he asked, trusting the man instinctively given his response to the news that someone needed help. The bearded and turbaned man walked out from behind the counter and strode purposefully to the back of the store where his pharmacy was. A few people had come into the store since the previous day and the news reports. Some he had hidden from, fearing the responses of the ignorant being directed at him.

Amrick Ali, commonly called Ricky as it was probably easier to accept his presence with an American sounding name, had lived in the United States for near on twenty years. Since the terror attacks of 2001 he had noticed a marked difference in the way people perceived him and his family. For starters, he was an Indian Sikh and not an Arab or Muslim as people nearly always assumed. He enjoyed a drink, and endured the constant comments like, *"Hey, I thought your kind didn't drink,"* and *"Isn't that against your religion?"*

He was not a radicalized terrorist, nor did he believe in any loss of life being justified. He enjoyed his work, and he kept his head down to keep the people of the small town in check with their medication. He was accepted on the whole, but he was always wary. Now, having seen the reports of the terror attacks all over the continent, he was grateful for the first time that his wife and children had returned to his native Kashmir to visit relatives. They had been gone a little over two weeks, and he doubted he would ever see them again. His reverie was interrupted as the small bell above the door jingled again and the two men brought in a young woman who seemed lethargic and confused.

"Sit her down there," Amrick told them, indicating a row of plastic seats. He walked into the aisles of his drug supply, snatching up things as he went from the places he knew they would be. He returned to the customer side of the counter and leaned down to put his face close to Louise's. Gently taking her left hand, he selected the ring finger and held it up before a small snapping sound produced a dot of blood on her fingertip. Holding a device with a protruding piece of paper to the blood he waited a few seconds with a furrowed brow.

"Please," he said to Jake over his left shoulder, "go to aisle four and bring back a bottle of Coca-Cola." Jake left without a word. "Make sure it's the real deal," Amrick shouted to him, "and not that sugar-free stuff."

"Got it," yelled Jake over the sound of his boots on the shiny shop floor.

Cal watched as the man in the turban tore open the packaging on another box and produced what looked like a small epipen. As Jake returned with a warm can of soda, Amrick rolled up the sleeve of Louise's top and jabbed the small needle into her arm.

She didn't flinch, whether that was because she had pierced her own skin so many times or whether she was crashing again Cal had no idea. Amrick gripped the ring pull and popped open the can before turning it and encouraging Louise to sip from it.

"The sugary drink will speed up the process," he told them. "When she is stabilized she will be able to manage it herself, at least I imagine so at her age," he said. Leaving Louise sipping at the drink autonomously, Amrick straightened and spoke to the others.

"My name is Amrick Ali," he said. "I am the pharmacist here."

"Jake Peters," Jake answered, "NYPD. This is Cal, he's English."

Why Jake had to add Cal's country of origin every time he introduced him made Cal furrow his brow; it was as though the cop was apologizing in advance for anything he might say or do, like he would suddenly produce a bowler hat and an umbrella.

"It is a pleasure to meet you both," Amrick answered. "Most people call me Ricky, and I suppose I have grown accustomed to being called this."

"How come you're still here?" Jake asked him, getting straight to the point. Now that they were deeper inside the store it was obvious that at least one group of people had raided it for supplies. He thought it strange that the pharmacist stayed behind when others had already left town.

"My wife and children have returned to India," he told them, his eyes casting down, "and I am ashamed to admit that I have never learned to drive." He finished lamely with his hands held open in an apologetic gesture.

That explained a lot. An awkward silence hung amongst the three men, as though Ricky's inability to drive was a matter of collective embarrassment.

"You should come with us," said a quiet voice from lower down. All three men turned to regard the expectant face of Louise, which now showed something resembling its true sparkle of her normal nature. Both Jake and Cal turned back to face him.

"I have no idea where you are going," he said, "but I believe my chances of doing any good here are small." He flashed his brilliantly white teeth at them; such an infectious smile that both men returned it through simple cognitive programming to respond that way to another person's happiness.

Saturday 2 p.m. - Ripley, WV

"Understood," Drew Briar said into his satellite phone and hung up without saying anything else. Madeline Tanner didn't wait for him to relay whatever news he had just received in his own time, and stalked toward him. She was mindful not to take out her fears and frustrations on the head of her security detail, but also wasn't of a mind to wait any longer than she had to. They were holed up in the town diner, the three blacked out SUVs with their blue and red lights having drawn some attention from the locals.

"Ma'am," Drew said, his face a shade paler than when he had taken the call. "I've just spoken with what's left of the military command. Whoever is attacking us is targeting all known military sites, and most of our communication network has been shut down along with power grids in most states." He paused, knowing that the information he would have to give her got worse and infinitely more important. "Satellite communications are currently our only viable network, but we have no way of knowing how long that will last."

"And?" Madeline said, knowing that there was more to come. "What else?"

"There are high-level assets in the state," he told her, not going into any details as he had few, but he knew that the NSA communications site hidden in the mountains was most likely where that last call had originated from. "Assets have been deployed to the air force base in Charlestown, which are currently not responding to any communications, and will be en route here to extract you."

"Extract me to where?" she asked.

"A safe site, ma'am," he said, "but that's not all …"

"Go on," Madeline said, narrowing her eyes as he seemed almost embarrassed.

"Ma'am," he said, raising his eyes to hers where she suspected there may be a glint of wetness. "Washington is gone, completely, and you need to be sworn in as soon as possible."

"Sworn in? Wh—" She stopped, the realization dawning on her.

"Madame President," Drew said formally, "these circumstances hardly dictate congratulations, but I'm honored to be at your service."

Madeline Tanner, soon to be the first female President of the United States of America, and in the midst of a surprise war being waged on civilians with the worst casualty rate of any conflict in history, sat her ass down on a seat and let that shock wash over her like a flood.

"Well, shiiit," she exclaimed breathlessly.

SNATCH AND GRAB

Saturday 2:10 p.m. - Greenbrier Mountains

"Let's go," Troy said, "wheels up in five."

The team had pored over the plans for their mission and waited for the word to go. Not thirty seconds after he had hung up the satellite phone was the first helicopter sparking into violent life and powering up. He had chosen to split the team, both the operators and the air assets. He now piled out the front door of the bunker with four of his team, taking both of their Black Hawks under the escort of a single Apache. This split of the team meant that he would be operating without a fire team partner, but it also meant leaving behind Chalky and the other four operators who could still be an effective fighting unit if his entire deployment didn't make it back. It also meant taking all of their aircraft which could carry troops, but he hoped to rectify that and bring back more than they left with.

Troy, climbing aboard the helicopter with Valdez and Farrell sat opposite Bones and Ghost, turned to give a thumbs-up to Gina Pilloni in the right-hand seat of the other Black Hawk. He switched his glance up to see that the Apache had already surged skywards under the control of Buck and Healey.

Pulling on his headset handed to him by the loadmaster of his bird as they climbed in altitude, he called out on the squad net for his three helicopters.

"Flight time is two-five minutes," he said, "repeat, two-five until we are on site." With that he sat back and closed his eyes, trying to visualize the ground he was heading for. Air force bases all over America, hell all over the world, were built the same way and if you've seen one, then you've pretty much seen them all. He hoped they would only be on the ground for a few minutes; after years of operating in obscure sandboxes and mostly in the dark, he felt like an alien walking around in full war gear in the daylight, and never before on US soil.

He hadn't told everyone the full extent of his orders—need to know and all that shit—but mostly he hadn't told them the rest because he didn't want anyone thinking that they had to do their job any different than they normally did.

Saturday 2:34 p.m. - Outside Charlestown, WV

The Apache flew ahead a half mile and circled the base once, radioing back that they saw nothing to raise any concerns. Flying straight in and flaring to land on the tarmac by the main building, the rotors of the two Black Hawks stayed turning ready to power up and lift at a moment's notice. Troy and his team dropped their boots onto the dry blacktop and spread out professionally. Anything heading their way would, hopefully, be detected by the space-age array of sensors on the Apache which loitered menacingly way above their heads. Heading straight for the doorway of the nearest building, weapon up and approaching heel toe, heel toe, Troy stopped as the door opened before he could get there.

The terrified eyes of the young man who opened it burned brightly, before the door slammed again. Troy, half expecting a response like this, threw himself to the wall beside the door and glanced back to see his team of four had similarly dispersed.

"Captain Gardner, US Army," he yelled through the closed door, mindful that their appearance was not that of a regular unit. Not by a long shot. "We're here on orders," he yelled, "coming in, DO NOT FIRE ON US." The last instruction boomed out in a voice which cut through the rotor noise and burned into the very souls of younger, less experienced men. Chalky often teased him for this trait of his, calling it his *Alpha* voice which other members of their pack were powerless to resist.

He reached a hand to the door, opened it a crack, and stepped back. No shots came, so he slowly entered. The contrast between the bright light of the afternoon sun and the dark, dingy interior of a ready room with little natural light took him a second to adjust to. He made out four, five faces in the shadows all looking at him in fear.

"Stand down," he told them, lowering his rifle barrel to point toward the dirty carpet and standing straight, "we're here to help."

Slowly, nervously, four men and a woman appeared from behind cover. Cover was a relative term, seeing as how ducking down behind a sofa was all well and good for a game of hide and seek, but about as effective as covering your eyes if you were expecting incoming bullets.

The base, as far as US military bases went, was small. He didn't have the luxury of time to explain the A to Z of their current predicament, so he cut right to the point.

"Any other personnel on base?" he asked, as Bones and Ghost joined him after leaving Valdez and Farrell to set up a hurried defense outside. Heads shook.

"Any of you rated as pilots?" again, heads shook. "Aircrew? Maintenance?" Heads nodded in response to the last word. Not ideal, but not insurmountable.

"What aircraft are on station?" he asked, mindful not to snap and scare the wide-eyed support staff who looked at him as though a god of war had just appeared before them, even though that wasn't an entirely inaccurate description.

"Twin Hueys," said what appeared to be the oldest man there, who still seemed younger than Troy's thirty-six years, "primarily configured for transport and SAR."

"Good," Troy said, "ready to fly?"

Nods, albeit confused ones, replied to his question.

"Okay, load up personal gear and maintenance tools for immediate dust off," he said, walking back out of the room and hitting the transmit button on his radio as he looked at the nearest Black Hawk thirty paces away. The face in the right-side seat watched him.

"Pilots," he said, "any of you familiar with a Huey?" No answer came back, as all six of the pilots listening in either exchanged glances or rolled their eyes. There wasn't a helicopter jock in the entire US forces who couldn't pilot a Huey.

"Captain," came a female voice, "most Huey's are older than us. Yes, we all know how to fly them."

Feeling a little like an idiot, he watched the face of the pilot who had spoken shake slowly at the idiocy of his question. In that moment, he knew it was Gina Pilloni; their team's war-virgin, and he had handed her a tiny slither of authority over him by demonstrating a minor lack of knowledge. It wasn't so much that he minded looking like an idiot, but it was the fact that he had thought the question was a relevant one. Then again, he imagined the look he would give Gina if she asked him if he was rated to use an AK47 instead of his customary SCAR.

Yeah, okay, he thought, *dumb question.*

"Good," he said, recovering, "co-pilots on me to fly two more birds." He walked back inside to find that Bones and Ghost had encouraged the remaining crew to move their asses. As the three operators helped the five ground crews collect their gear and tools as well as prepare the two light gray Huey helicopters for immediate departure, they learned that most of the base personnel was comprised of auxiliary soldiers. When the bombs started falling, many had simply evaporated to their homes, but the brass had taken off without letting anyone else know where they were going. History was irrelevant to Troy, and he half expected to be warned of incoming aircraft at any moment to bomb this base as so many others had been hit. Gina and the other co-pilot, Nick Jenkins, hurried though pre-flight checks and sparked their engines to life. Troy hit the transmit button again.

"Valdez, Farrell, back to the chopper," he said, pausing to receive a brief acknowledgement of the order. "Jenkins, take the base personnel back to the bunker. Hammond, escort them," he said, sending one of their Black Hawks back to base. "Pilloni, Taylor," he said, calling the crew which had carried his team and were now split flying a helicopter each, "we continue to a second objective. Apache with us. Acknowledge."

A round of acknowledgments fired in sequence in his ear; the benefit of being a small unit commander with dedicated air support being that he recognized each voice without the rigma-role of lengthy call signs. Call signs were great when working outside of his team, but for this they simply weren't needed, and in the Special Forces world something which is unnecessary and slows you down is ditched. Now, having split his team, he introduced a degree of separation.

From the bird's eye view which Colonel Simon and Major Healey enjoyed, the four birds spun up and lifted off, one black and one gray heading east, and an identical pair heading due north. Troy hit the transmit button again.

"Endeavor Actual with Endeavor One and Two en route to secondary objective," he said. "Bunker, are you receiving?" A split-second pause before Dillon's voice came back to him from their base. "Endeavor actual, Bunker. Acknowledged and awaiting Endeavor Three and Four to return. Confirm Apache with Endeavor Actual."

"Apache confirms," came a female voice, "call us Hawk."

Troy had to smile at the all-round show of bravado, as the five birds split up and went two separate ways.

Saturday 3:04 p.m. - Ripley, WV

"Understood," Drew said again before hanging up the satellite phone and prompting a wave of déjà-vu for Madeline. "Our ride is inbound, ma'am," he said, reaching to speak into his personal radio and repeating the information to the four agents deployed to protect the secluded diner. "ETA five minutes." Drew hadn't checked, but he assumed they would have enough room to take the principle, *Hell, the soon to be president*, he thought, as well as her aide and the six Secret Service agents.

Five minutes went by in a blur, and the rotor noise was audible before the aircraft came into view between the tall trees either side of the road. The parking lot was big enough, despite the three armored SUVs parked there, for a pair of helicopters to set down long enough for three armed and fiercely wild-looking soldiers to drop out. Troy ran to the door, indicated for them to get their asses on the aircraft by way of waving them forward and directing them with a bladed hand toward the light gray helicopter. Six dark-suited agents formed a tight pack around two women and moved as a single organism toward the helicopter. They climbed aboard, and Troy pointed toward the headsets with attached boom mics. With their passengers safely aboard, Troy and his two operators jumped back onboard their Black Hawk, and once again under the ever-watchful eye of their own personal Hawk, dusted off. The noses of the helicopters all dipped and their tails raised to propel them eastwards, toward the distant mountain. The radio burst to life in Troy's ear.

"To whom am I speaking?" said a female voice, richly cultured and accented. Troy had to assume that was the principle he was tasked to retrieve and protect.

"Captain Troy Gardner, ma'am," he said. "US Army Special Forces."

"Captain Gardner," came the response, "I, and my people, are grateful for your assistance."

"Ma'am," Troy said back, "we're all your people now." A few glances were shot at him in the back of their helicopter, and he assumed now was as good a time as any to let everyone know what they had just achieved.

"Bunker, Endeavor Actual," he called into the radio, "be advised Endeavor Two is now Air Force One." The silence in response was answer enough to the gravity of the situation, regardless of the slight inaccuracies of the call sign.

"Acknowledged, Endeavor Actual. Bunker awaiting safe arrival of Air Force One. Out."

LONG ROAD AHEAD

Saturday 4:38 p.m. - Pennsylvania Turnpike, Somerset

"We can't stay on the highway like this," Louise said as she leaned through to the front seat. The roads were getting busier now, with people heading in all directions driving overloaded cars. "Head south from here," she told Jake, "we can cut across country."

The conversation to accept Ricky into their small group was a short one, and Louise had made her feelings clear from the outset. He turned out to be easy company, making any natural silence feel comfortable as they travelled along deep in their own thoughts.

The overwhelming deluge of cars heading in the opposite direction told a story by itself, as Pittsburgh and the surrounding towns disgorged their human contents to scatter the population to the wind. The four of them had driven all afternoon, stopping only once to siphon gasoline from abandoned cars. Mob rule had taken over everywhere; the inescapable element of human nature seeing everyone and everything as either prey or predator. Many others, just as they were, brandished their hunting rifles and shotguns as a means to dissuade anyone from trying to take what was theirs, and the sense of human cooperation had disintegrated when applied to strangers.

Turning away from the masses and taking the smaller roads added time to their journey, but made for safer passage. Their pickup was relatively new, and they were well equipped with both weapons, supplies and medicines after taking everything they could carry from Ricky's store.

Cal thought that what he saw was the opposite of how the Brits had faced any attack in the past, even though the current concept was only applicable to the Blitz of World War II. In British history, when faced with attack, his ancestors would congregate in large towns to rely on the strength of walls and numbers. They would cooperate.

He imagined if the UK was suffering the same fate. If they were reeling from nuclear strikes in London, Manchester, Liverpool, Birmingham. If they were hunkering down and watching the fate of the United States of America on television, or if they too were grabbing their belongings and heading for the hills to disappear and disassociate with the populated areas. His personal reverie was disrupted by the sight of an overturned station wagon with a wheel still spinning. They rolled past slowly, seeing nobody with the wreck and no signs of anyone nearby.

"We should keep moving," Ricky offered from the back seat next to Louise, a hint of nervous tension in his voice, "it is likely that people will use such things to try and make us stop."

That observation went unanswered. None of them were that surprised how quickly mob rule took over, but all of them were quietly horrified how fast it happened and how quickly a fellow human being would resort to animalistic violence when facing the terrifying prospects they all imagined. Picking up their speed again, Jake nursed the pickup along the winding roads gaining and losing elevation in contrast to the long, straight highways they had been traveling on before.

Saturday, 5 p.m. - Cuba

One thousand and three hundred miles south, dull green troop transport planes stacked up on the runways for their turn to take off. Plane after plane rammed with as many troops as could be carried jostled for their uncomfortable space onboard to await the even more uncomfortable and deafening journey north east where they took care to skirt the area of radioactive destruction which had been Florida.

The People's Liberation Army had transported almost a hundred thousand troops to Cuba and Venezuela over the last month, all carried by routine cargo ships and none of them arousing the suspicion of the world's intelligence community.

272

The Chinese troops themselves had not been told where they were going, for fear of them telling anyone. Without warning, entire regiments of soldiers were shipped without affording them the opportunity to contact anyone they knew. They were spirited away by night, boarded onto ships or flown out of the country. Fifty thousand more were aboard troop transport ships, as three quarters of the Chinese Navy steamed toward the western seaboard.

The first wave of the invasion was underway. Dozens of planes headed for Texas, New Mexico, and Colorado. There they would seize control of the military assets which had been softened, if not crippled, by the aerial bombardment which had been raining destruction on the United States almost constantly since the fuse had been lit.

Other units were sent further north to seize control of sensitive infrastructure the leadership felt was necessary for their plans, as well as to shut major transport links and control the movement of anyone who survived the aerial campaign and the nuclear attacks. The plan was to drive the surviving occupants to the center of the continent, and there to control them.

~

"It is the duty of the citizen's militias to protect and defend the unalienable rights of all members of their communities. The members of the Appalachian Militia shall ever stand accountable, as have our forefathers before us. First to God, from whom we acknowledge the authority of all rights, and then unto our fellow citizens of our native sovereign states," Reverend Jackson Charles Harris said proudly to his congregation. His militia was sometimes more of a church than a people's army, and he tried hard to keep the focus of his flock on the righteous path.

"We attest that all power is inherent in the people, that governments, being instituted for the common benefit, the doctrine of non-resistance against arbitrary power is absurd, slavish, and destructive of the good and happiness of mankind." That part was less popular, as a number of his people were anti-government.

"We pledge to promote and defend the unalienable God-given rights of all citizens" —he raised his voice as he shook a fist toward the rafters and received a rolling growl of agreement from his assembly— "regardless of race, sex or national origin, as is expressed in the United States Constitution and the Bill of Rights." He dropped his hand, scanned the room, and made eye contact with as many as he could to build the tension in the room.

"We pledge to repel foreign aggression and invasions." He had to pause as the growl became a roar of agreement punctuated by shouts of *Amen.* "By preparing and training for defense and by our encouraging and showing reason why all citizens should stand stoutly against all forms of tyranny."

Reverend Harris leaned back, his hands gripping tightly to the altar from where he preached his sermon. The people before him, men, women, and children, roared their support and approval for his words. He suspected that so many of his militia had been praying for such an occurrence for many years. The second amendment was their God-given right for exactly this reason. They had watched on screens, learning of the fate of the rest of the United States, though the amount of news channels that were still broadcasting was getting fewer by the hour. He had called everyone to attend when he had seen footage of parachutes—hundreds of them—opening high over the mountains and hills of his native east Kentucky. They had yet to find out who was invading their blessed United States of America, but they sure as hell weren't going to wait to find out.

They were going to war.

Saturday 6:21 p.m. - Near Parkersburg, WV

After another tense stop to try and buy fuel from a gas station, the four occupants of the dark Ford pickup decided against contact with other people unless they couldn't avoid it. They drove on, leaving the carnage and the fights behind, and stopped to siphon gas from parked cars. The traffic had eased off to only the occasional car after they had abandoned the major roads to head across country, and the tension rose every time a car drove up on them fast and passed them. Loaded cars were heading the other way, and one station wagon with possessions tied to the roof flashed its lights at them frantically. Slowing on instinct, Jake asked the others what he should do.

"Pull up, see what they want," Louise said. Jake looked to Cal who nodded agreement but drew the Glock just in case. He slowed and wound down the electric window as Cal leaned over ready to bring the weapon to bear.

"Don't go that way!" the driver of the station wagon yelled before he'd even stopped. "There's roadblocks on the highway."

"Law enforcement?" Jake asked, confused and hopeful at the same time.

"No idea, man," yelled back the driver, waving at the woman in the passenger seat beside him to keep back from his window. "Army, but not ours. They're shooting at people, man, turn around!" With that, he gunned the engine and the car surged away.

The four of them looked at each other until Ricky broke the silence.

"He sounded crazy," he said carefully, "but that doesn't mean he isn't right."

"Roadblocks seem right," Jake said, "but neither army or law enforcement would fire on people unless they had to. I say we check it out."

There was neither agreement nor disagreement in the car, so Jake rolled forward and picked up speed. They sat in silence for the few minutes it took for the next town to come into view. Jake avoided the ramp to join the highway and cruised into the town. All eyes were scanning, the faint noises of disorder coming in vague waves through the windows.

"JAKE!" Louise screamed, pointing her finger frantically ahead. Jake's eyes shot back to the front, reacting instinctively as his foot automatically switched from the gas pedal to the brake. His brain only registered the appearance of two human shapes ahead in the road, and the cognitive process hadn't yet registered that those two shapes were pointing weapons at them. The cognitive process hadn't yet assimilated and deciphered the meaning of the two shapes wearing uniform, hadn't yet understood the demeanor and stance, couldn't yet explain to him what it all meant when put together.

He may not have fully understood it, nor could he have put into words what made him respond differently, but the same subconscious process which had made him react to Louise's shout now kicked in and overrode his body's response by slamming his foot back down hard on the gas pedal. The competing noise of shouts and screams from inside the cab of their truck merged into one cacophonous din of pure panic, punctuated only by the sound of the two shapes slamming into the truck's grille and bouncing away. The truck was too high and the shapes too short to be thrown up into the windshield to roll over them but were instead pummeled down to the tarmac where they were both crushed by the big wheels; the truck bouncing horrifically over the broken bodies.

The screams and shouts didn't abate as they carried on forwards, Jake himself yelling out loud as he gripped the wheel in terror and shock at what he just done. The back window of the cab burst inwards with a wickedly sharp crack as the windshield instantly starburst around the large hole showing between Cal and Jake. The sound of the bullet passing through left their ears ringing but remarkably left their bodies unhurt. Jake kept his foot down hard, covering three blocks in a straight line before he had to slow to negotiate the wreckage of a burning car. Bodies littered the road and the sounds of gunfire could be heard from an alarmingly short distance away. Jake's eyes were wild, trying to see in every direction at once as the ungodly surge of adrenaline he had just had dumped into his bloodstream dialed up his senses and reactions to previously unknown levels. It didn't last long as, although his eyes were scanning wildly for threats, he failed to see the truck of a similar size coming from his right as he blasted through the last small intersection before the Ohio River came into view.

SO HELP ME GOD

Saturday 7:08 p.m. - Bunker, Greenbrier Mountains

Endeavor had returned to the bunker within an hour of the first helicopters sent back. The aircraft were landed and checked over by their team of four mechanics. The last of the five rescued personnel were aircrew and, as such, had lacked current employment so were assigned to sort gear and keep the coffee machine in optimal condition. The secret service team were assigned a bunk area to themselves, but their principal was shown to a set of rooms which were technically designed for the base commander, like the captain's quarters in a warship. Madeline and her aide, introduced to Troy as Lillie, were given the interlocking rooms.

Farrell and Valdez volunteered themselves to better arm the secret service team, breaking open the store room to them and handing out tactical clothing as well as six of the brand new HK416 CQB—or close quarter battle—models. These carried the full weight 5.56 NATO ammo, which came with red dot sights and were configured in ten-inch barrel mode for use in confined spaces. It was the modern peak of assault rifle technology coming in a sub-machine gun sized package. Troy found

Dillon at their command center and introduced him to the head of the secret service detail.

"Dillon," he said as he walked in, "this is Agent-in-charge Briar." The two shook hands and Drew Briar tried to place Dillon's role in the team. They were obviously Delta, that much was plain to any former serviceman given their irregular uniform and weapon choices, and made firm in his mind by the assortment of beards on display; no regular military unit would allow such a wild look. Dillon seemed different to him; smaller and more meticulous as he was the only one of the team who still shaved every day, even if he was wearing a day's worth of stubble by that point.

"Drew," he said, shaking Dillon's hand as he rose from the chair to greet him. "Marine Corps, retired obviously."

"Same, brother," Dillon told him. "I was F.A.S.T," he said, pronouncing it 'fast.' Drew's eyebrows raised. The Fleet Antiterrorist Security Teams of the United States Marine Corps were a small unit tasked primarily with high-value target protection, and many in the services thought of them as privileged security guards. Drew had served with a guy who was recruited and never seen by his old unit again. Drew didn't need to say that he was impressed by Dillon or any of others, and to say so out loud would make him seem like an excited kid. Troy left the two of them to run over the facts as they knew them and picked up the last message from the remaining elements of command. He had already heard the news, but reading the facts made it seem worse than he thought.

```
Endeavor eyes only:
Nuclear   attacks   confirmed   on   both
eastern and western seaboards by mis-
sile and air bombardment. Targets of
populations centers. Reports of aerial
insertion   from   south   America   con-
firmed,   all   states   not   directly   af-
fected by nuclear attack are reporting
hostile forces engaging civilians and
officials. Await orders for targets
and report all intelligence.
```

Drew knew this, and was eager to get back on the ground to test the resolve of these hostile forces to see if they could handle Endeavor as well as they could handle civilians. He confidently doubted they could. The second paragraph was what really took his breath. On a separate sheet were some printed words which he was to get Madeline Tanner to read aloud in the presence of all witnesses available.

```
Endeavor Actual:
Conduct inauguration ceremony of Pres.
Tanner at your earliest possible.
```

Jesus, thought Troy, *they want me to do it?* But there wasn't anyone else, least not anyone in charge and no Congress or

White House to do it at any more. Their bunker was now effectively their nation's capital. Turning to Dillon to ask him how to use the bunker's announcement system, he grabbed up the mic and depressed his thumb on the switch.

"All personnel," he said, his voice echoing out along the underground halls of their fortress, "meet in the canteen" —he flipped over his wrist to check his watch— "at nineteen-thirty hours. No exceptions. Gardner out." Then he left to go and knock on the door of the rooms which should, in essence, be assigned to him.

~

"Come on in," came the rich, accented voice from behind the wooden door.

He opened the handle and squeezed himself through the doorframe, feeling giant in the confined space with the two smaller women inside. Troy still hadn't removed his full war gear, nor was he likely to unless he stood down for any length of time, which he guessed wouldn't be any time soon.

"Ma'am," he said formally, feeling brutish with his array of weapons and heavy body armor. "I'm sure you heard the announcement?"

"I did, Captain, and I thank you," Madeline said as she rose to stand before him. She was not a short woman, but she had to crane her neck at that distance to meet the eyes of the man who stood at a shade over six foot two, but was just one of those generally big all over people.

"I need to give you this to read out in front of everyone," he said, handing her the separate sheet of paper he had pulled from the printer. Her eyes scanned it, seeing the familiar words which she knew by heart but was sure she would forget if she had to read them herself for real, and thanked him again.

"Troy?" she said to his retreating back as it blocked the artificial light from the corridor.

"Ma'am?" he asked turning back, pleased that she had quickly learned to drop the formality of rank when talking to him.

She opened her mouth but no words came out. She seemed lost in thought for the right way to say what she meant, to convey all her feelings and emotions, but she couldn't find the words.

"You'll be fine, ma'am," Troy reassured her. "If you'll excuse me, I need to see if any of my devils own a Bible."

~

Troy knew exactly where he would find a Bible, and sure as anything their resident jumper produced it from a pouch and handed it to him as soon as he asked. Bruce, as he was known simply because his last name was Lee and he trained in martial arts, never went anywhere without the battered, leather-bound book. Where other soldiers would grab ten minute's shut-eye whenever they could, Bruce liked to leaf through the thin pages carefully and find references to the everyday things he saw in the Scriptures. He said it gave him peace to know that he and Jesus saw the same things in life, even if Jesus didn't specialize in jumping out of aircraft and finding new ways to get to earth safely in war zones.

With the book in one hand, he stood facing the smaller woman as their entire personnel gathered round them in the mess hall. He watched as she placed her left hand on the book and raised her right.

"I do solemnly swear," she said, swallowing and continuing in a louder, more authoritative voice, "that I will faithfully execute the office of the President of the United States, and will do to the best of my ability, preserve, protect and defend the Constitution of the United States of America." She swallowed again, giving a tiny shake of her head to flick an errant strand of hair away from her eyes, and fixed Troy's gaze with her own. *"So help me God,"* she finished.

And so help *him*, God, he believed her words and the conviction in her voice.

"Madame President," he said solemnly.

"Captain," she replied, a gleam in her eye.

~

At the northern tip of the state which now contained the first female president of the United States of America, four wet and shocked passengers drifted south on the Ohio river. The blood from their cuts, sustained when their truck had caught the full impact of the collision just aft of the rear tires and spun them out violently, had been washed away by their panicked flight into the river.

Of all the supplies they had successfully recovered and carefully stacked into the truck, they had only managed to salvage their weapons, a couple of bags of food and water, and, luckily, the cooler stacked with insulin, which Louise clung on to as though her life depended on it.

It does, thought Cal as he saw her shiver and moved closer to put his arm around her for warmth and comfort. Her grip on the box didn't relax, but she rested her head on him.

The outboard motor which Ricky had managed to get running had lasted them for just over an hour before it spluttered into silence, and now they drifted as Jake tried to keep their slow course to the center of the wide waterway and away from the sides where other people and bad things were. Nobody spoke, because nobody knew what to say. They had been in the middle of a terror attack, seen the country devastated by nuclear explosions and bombing runs, seen anarchy and mob rule take over normal people and had now watched troops parachute to the ground where they tried to round up the population.

They were exhausted, scared, and they had little to no clue where they were headed. For now, drifting south on the Ohio River with enough food and water to last maybe two days, they were just happy enough to be away from land.

THE BEGINNING OF THE END

Sunday 00:03 a.m. Local Time, London

An emergency meeting of COBRA, or the UK's Cabinet Office Briefing Room to be long-winded as the British liked to be, was called late in the evening. The prime minister was surrounded by senior politicians, as well as the entire raft of armed forces high-ranking officers and their advisors. The doors were sealed shut, and the noise quickly faded away.

"Ladies and gentlemen," said the PM, "I'll hand over to the intelligence community for an up-to-date briefing before we begin."

A man stood and fastened the top button of his suit jacket smoothly with one hand; a practiced movement which was subconscious as much as it spoke of his upbringing in a polite, elitist society.

"As of yesterday, the North American continent is effectively cut off," he began. "Twelve nuclear explosions have been detected and fallout has begun to disperse according to prevailing winds. Also, precision bombing strikes have neutralized the majority of the armed forces response and some internet footage has found its way out which shows that an advance invasion force has begun to seize control of infrastructure across the country. We have not yet received any communication from the American government, however satellite imagery." He paused, glancing at another suited man who tapped at the keys of a laptop and brought up a picture to the large screen on the wall. "Shows that Washington D.C. has been destroyed."

He stopped speaking and glanced back to the PM, who nodded for him to sit. Effortlessly unfastening the button of his jacket with finger and thumb again, he took his seat.

"Our allies are under attack," the PM said, "and we do not yet know who is responsible. Can anyone answer that?"

Glances were exchanged and uniformed men shifted uncomfortably in their seats. The PM tried to retain some dignity and not snap at them for an answer, but luckily for them a young man cleared his throat.

"Yes?" she said, fixing him with her gaze.

"Hetherington, ma'am. MI6," he said by way of introduction, before giving his explanation without further wasting anyone's time. "Our satellites picked this up a few hours ago," he said, hitting keys of his own computer and clicking through a series of low-resolution slides.

"Our intelligence sources indicate mass troop movement in both North Korea and China."

Silence descended once more, and the PM steepled her fingers with her elbows on the polished mahogany table.

"Get me confirmation," she said. "I need the UN on a conference call in an hour, and I want options to rescue citizens and discuss our ability to offer aid and counterstrikes."

As one, the combined cabinet and advisors took a breath. They were preparing to go to war.

Sunday 7:03 a.m. Local Time, Beijing

Dressed in a fresh black suit again, the woman who wore no insignia or identification paced around the control room looking over shoulders at displays as she went. Her uncle, the president of the republic, had cautioned her that he didn't want casualties. The reports she saw were not filling her with confidence that she would be able to report an inconsequential sum when she was next summoned to see him, and it seemed that all the meticulous planning had factored in every possibility bar one.

They had manipulated the rogue group of Americans into destabilizing the infrastructure and confusing any response to their initial attacks, and they had executed that first wave of devastation with close to a 100 percent success rate.

What they had failed to account for, what they should have realized was probably their biggest hurdle from the beginning, was one simple fact.

America would fight back.

ABOUT THE AUTHOR

Devon C Ford is from the UK and lives in the Midlands. His career in public services started in his teens and has provided a wealth of experiences, both good and some very bad, which form the basis of the books ideas that cause regular insomnia.

You can find more about the author:

Facebook: @decvoncfordofficial

Twitter: @DevonFordAuthor

Website: www.devoncford.com

After it Happened by Devon C Ford

Set in the UK in the immediate aftermath of a mysterious illness which swept the country and left millions dead, the series follows the trials facing a reluctant hero, Dan, and the group that forms around him. They must battle the elements, find sufficient supplies and equipment to survive, and protect themselves against the most destructive force on the planet: other people.

www.vulpine-press.com/after-it-happened

Printed in Great Britain
by Amazon

81990424R00171